D0773008

You Know What Is Right

STORIES BY

Jim Heynen

1985

North Point Press · San Francisco

The author and publisher gratefully acknowledge the following magazines and anthologies, where some of these tales first appeared: *Aag Aag, Alcatraz 2, Chowder Review, Cutbank, Field, Georgia Review, Jeopardy, Kuksu, Luna Tack, Mississippi Mud, North American Review, Northwest Review, Outlaw, Pembroke Magazine, Poet and Critic, Poetry Now, Quarry West, Seattle Review, Slackwater Review, Willow Springs, Zero.*

For friends Bob and Linda Clifton

Contents

Part I

Eye to Eye

The boys liked to watch pigs being born. Drying them off in the straw. Putting them next to the sow's teats. Watching them discover the little world of the farrowing pen. But after a while the boys would get tired of this and go off to do something else.

Except for the youngest boy. He liked to stick around by himself. When the other boys left, he leaned down and put his face close to the sow. Now that there was no one there to laugh at him. This way he could hear the pig coming and when it was born his face was right over the newborn. He quickly put his eye over the eye of the little pig. When it opened its eye, the first thing it saw was the boy's eye, only an inch or two away from its own.

The boy stared into the pig's eye and the pig stared into the boy's. What the boy liked to see was the expression on

the pig's face. It was a look of surprise. But not a big surprise. Not the startled look of seeing something you didn't
expect to see—like a ghost or a creature from Mars. More
like the look of somebody waking up in the back seat of a car
who doesn't realize how far he's gone since he fell asleep.
The look that says, Oh, I didn't know we'd gone this far, but
okay.

Then the boy lifted his head so the pig could notice everything else. The pig knew what to do. Stand up, breathe,
look around for a nipple. The boy didn't try to keep the pig
from its business. He knew they both had their own worlds
to live in. That didn't change the fact that for a few seconds
they had been somewhere that nobody else would have to
know about.

❀

Yellow Girl

When drainage tile was put in the bottomlands, corn could be planted where only slough grass grew before. But the tile drained the pond too. The boys couldn't remember when ducks and bullheads swam there, but the pond was still surrounded by willow trees and made a good place to get away from everything. They'd go down to the pond and look for old bottles and badger holes, or they'd make dust castles out of the pond bed.

Then one year there was a big flood and the pond was back in spite of the drainage tile. When the waters went down, the boys went to the pond to see what it looked like with water in it. They brought fishing poles, figuring that where there was water there would be fish. Corn stalks and debris from all over the county were hanging in the willow trees around the pond and the pond was brimming with muddy water. They fished for an hour and now and then saw ripples in the water that told them something alive was in there. But they couldn't tell what.

Then one of the boys hooked something. It didn't fight much but it was big. His pole bent like a horseshoe. The boy managed to pull it towards the shore slowly. They were expecting a big mud turtle, and they had sticks ready. Then part of the catch showed itself on the surface, a large rolling motion, like a big fish turning over on its back as it swam.

I saw its yellow belly! shouted one of the boys. It's a giant catfish!

But it wasn't a catfish. It wasn't anything alive at all. It was a dirty dress the flood had brought from somewhere. The boys took it off the hook and laid it out on the shore. It was a girl's dress. When they squeezed the water out, they could see that it was yellow, with small red flowers. It had two pockets and white buttons at the neck. The boys tied the buttons and checked the pockets. They were empty.

The dress lay on the shore and the breeze started to dry it. The colors became clearer and brighter as it dried and the hem ruffled a little in the breeze.

As a joke one of the boys drew a head over the dress. The other boys joined in, scratching legs and arms in the soft dirt. There, one of them said. There is our yellow girl.

The boys left her lying there, knowing there was little chance that such a flood as the last one would come and wash her away. They went down to the pond often that summer, always saying they were going fishing. And they did catch a few small bullheads. The yellow girl stayed in place through the summer, and when the weather changed her at all the boys fixed her up again by retracing her head, arms, and legs in the dirt. They came to think of her as their sleeping beauty, though none of them stooped to kiss her.

Pocket
Gopher Feet

You could turn in a pocket gopher's front feet at the bank. There was a bounty of twenty cents a pair. The feet had to be dry or in salt. Just so they didn't stink up the place.

Getting the bounty on pocket gopher feet was not easy money. The boys set a dozen traps every night. Digging down under the mound to find the crossroads. Then scraping out a little nest to put the trap in and closing everything up airtight so the pocket gopher couldn't tell that somebody had booby-trapped its back yard.

The boys didn't mind so much if they caught a mean one. The kind that digs itself out, following the chain to the stake outside, and sits there waiting for you, hissing, one foot in the trap but ready to take on the world with its two long front teeth. This was the easy kind, and the boys put a mean pocket gopher out of its misery quickly with a baseball bat.

The bad kind were the ones that wanted to get away. One of these might pack the dirt around the trap so hard that the boys would have a hard time pulling the trap out. Or it might set its three free legs into the dirt so deep that the boys would have to pull so hard that they pulled the trapped foot right off. Or one of this kind might beat the boys to the punch by chewing its foot off and leaving it there in the trap before the boys got there.

So what do you do with one pocket gopher foot?

Just because a pocket gopher wanted to live so bad that it pulled or chewed one of its feet off didn't stop the boys from trying to get their money. The first time it happened, the boys brought the one foot in for the bounty, thinking that the woman in the bank wouldn't notice. She did. Where's the other foot? she said.

We only caught one foot, said the youngest boy.

Sorry, said the woman. The bounty is for both feet.

Couldn't we get half a bounty for this foot? asked another one of the boys. The woman would hear nothing of it. So the boys saved the foot and the next time a gopher left one foot in a trap, they put it in a little sack with the first one and brought the two feet in for the bounty. They figured the woman in the bank wouldn't notice that they were not a perfect match. She did. These feet don't match, she said.

My socks don't match either, said the youngest boy, but these are both my feet.

Look, said the woman, moving the mismatched pocket gopher feet around with the end of a pencil. They're both right front feet. No bounty for these. And I will thank you if you do not try to fool me again.

The boys realized the county knew what it was doing when they hired the woman in the bank to take care of pocket gopher bounties. They went home with their mismatched pocket gopher feet. They didn't throw them away. They knew there was a slim chance that they might catch the other foot of those pocket gophers some day. The odds weren't very good, but they seemed better than trying to fool the bank woman who had an awfully good eye for spotting counterfeits.

The Youngest Boy

It was not easy being the youngest boy. Being the last one in the race to the house for supper. Being the one who held the wrenches while the others fixed the bicycle. Being the one no one would believe when everyone else was lying. And the one who could not back his anger with muscle.

But there was an advantage to being small. Some nights, very late, when he wanted the world to himself, he slipped out of bed with such small noises that no one heard. And he moved through the house making sounds that the rats or wind might make. Then, he waited until the wind changed enough to move the metal fan on the windmill so that it squeaked. At the same time, he opened the screen door and the two squeaks went together and he was outside. Here there were always some animal sounds, and it was easy to fit them in with the sounds of his walking and overall legs rubbing. Steers rubbing against wooden fences because the grubs in their backs did not sleep at night. Or sick pigs that had swallowed wire plodding to the drinking trough to quench the burning in their stomachs. Even birds and chickens with their little fluttering pains. With his flashlight still turned off, he went down to the barn and the door with new hinges which didn't squeak. Inside, he turned on the flashlight and shone it in the faces of calves who got up to see what there was to eat, then lay down again, watching him but not expecting anything. He made up little songs and sang to them as they lay in the hay content, not listening to him but not complaining either.

What Happened During the Ice Storm

One winter there was a freezing rain. How beautiful! people said when things outside started to shine with ice. But the freezing rain kept coming. Tree branches glistened like glass. Then broke like glass. Ice thickened on the windows until everything outside blurred. Farmers moved their livestock into the barns, and most animals were safe. But not the pheasants. Their eyes froze shut.

Some farmers went ice-skating down the gravel roads with clubs to harvest pheasants that sat helplessly in the roadside ditches. The boys went out into the freezing rain to find pheasants too. They saw dark spots along a fence. Pheasants, all right. Five or six of them. The boys slid their feet along slowly, trying not to break the ice that covered the snow. They slid up close to the pheasants. The pheasants pulled their heads down between their wings. They couldn't tell how easy it was to see them huddled there.

The boys stood still in the icy rain. Their breath came out in slow puffs of steam. The pheasants' breath came out in quick little white puffs. Some of them lifted their heads and turned them from side to side, but they were blindfolded with ice and didn't flush. The boys had not brought clubs, or sacks, or anything but themselves. They stood over the pheasants, turning their own heads, looking at each other, each expecting the other to do something. To pounce on a pheasant, or to yell Bang! Things around them were shining and dripping with icy rain. The barbed wire fence. The fence posts. The broken stems of grass. Even the grass seeds. The grass seeds looked like little yolks inside gelatin whites. And the pheasants looked like unborn birds glazed in egg white. Ice was hardening on the boys' caps and coats. Soon they would be covered with ice too.

Then one of the boys said, Shh. He was taking off his coat, the thin layer of ice splintering in flakes as he pulled his arms from the sleeves. But the inside of the coat was dry and warm. He covered two of the crouching pheasants with his coat, rounding the back of it over them like a shell. The other boys did the same. They covered all the helpless pheasants. The small gray hens and the larger brown cocks. Now the boys felt the rain soaking through their shirts and freezing. They ran across the slippery fields, unsure of their footing, the ice clinging to their skin as they made their way toward the warm blurry lights of the house.

Dehorning

Nothing could be worse than dehorning cattle. Not just the blood which covered their faces and ran down over their eyes and nostrils. Not just the sound of the saw cutting through the base of the horn. Not just the metal dehorning chute wedging against the sides of the animal and holding its head between the two bars. And not just the bellowing and snorting of the animal as it tried to pull free. But all of these together.

Sometimes the boys tried to act brave by standing around waiting for the horns to fall to the ground. Or they would hold the ointments and salves that were supposed to stop the bleeding when the job was done. But sooner or later the dehorning would get to be too much for them and they would find an excuse to walk away.

If they went off to the grove to play on their model farm,

they took turns pretending they were a steer being de-horned. One would get down on his knees. Another would hold triangles of wood scrap on his skull. Another would use a wood file as a saw. Together they made the sounds of dehorning while the wood scraps were being cut off.

Doing this, the boys learned what cattle went through. They learned that the animal can see the horns sticking out from its head, hard pieces of its own body that turned whichever way its head turned, that could be used to keep other animals away or to rip hay loose from a bale. The boys learned what it felt like to see one horn fall to the ground and then see the dehorner move with his saw to the other side for the one that was left. Sometimes they poured water over the head of the one being dehorned so that he could also learn what it felt like to have blood running down his fore-head, into his eyes and nostrils.

Playing the dehorning game didn't make watching de-horning any easier. But it did make the chores of feeding the cattle and pitching their manure, even in cold weather, much easier.

What the
Boys Did about
the Lightning

One stormy night a neighbor went outside to look at the sky. He stood under a clothesline. That was his mistake. He was struck by lightning and died.

The boys went to his funeral and, looking up at his face in the coffin, they saw that the insides of his nostrils were black. Not even the undertaker's powder and creams could hide what the lightning had done.

That was how the boys learned to hate thunder. It was thunder that sounded so interesting that the man walked out into the night where the lightning could find him. But the boys also heard the grown-ups talking about rubber. If only he had been wearing thick rubber boots, someone said. Rubber could have saved him.

That was all the boys needed to hear. They rolled rubber tires out of the grove where they were rotting under the huckleberries. They put a tire where people might go when they heard the thunder. They put one against the clothes-line pole to protect anyone who might walk out like the dead man did when he heard the thunder call. They leaned two of them against their house. That whole pile of old tires found new places to rot. Where they could do some good. The boys told everyone why they put the tires everywhere. So no one moved them.

To make sure that they were safe themselves, they brought one tire up into their room and set it in the window like a big wreath. Through the circle of that tire they watched and listened to many storms roar through the sky and pass them safely by.

The Globe
and Anthill
Joke

One boring summer day the boys sneaked the globe out of the front room and took it outside in the sun. Now all the countries and mountains and rivers looked brighter. Almost like real places. The boys sat down around the globe talking. Wondering if they would ever go anyplace besides the farm. Or town. Or the river. They wondered if they would ever see New York or Old Faithful.

They rolled the globe around in the grass and took turns stopping it with their forefingers, pretending that wherever they stopped it would be a place they would get to go someday. One stopped it on the islands of Micronesia, another on Istanbul, another on Toronto, one on the Sahara Desert. They went on doing this for a long time. Then one boy pointed at the ground. Look! Just under the globe were two ants dragging a big dead beetle. The globe was in their way but they kept pushing and pulling. Sometimes they tried to move the globe and sometimes the beetle. They kept at it and the boys kept watching. Pretty soon they had moved the beetle an inch. Then another inch. The boys leaned with the ants the way people lean with players at a football game. They saw the anthill about three feet away. Two hours later the boys were still watching and the ants were halfway to the anthill.

Then one of the boys took the globe and set it on the anthill where the ants were headed with their big catch.

There! he said. We did our part. The ants went on plodding in their usual way, while the boys laughed and laughed at the joke they had played on them.

What Started
Driving the Cows
into the Barn

The boys joked about how different people looked like different animals. But then one day as they were driving the cows into the barn, they noticed how different cows looked like different people.

It started when one of the boys said, Hey, look! this one has a swayback just like old man Dikstra. They all laughed when they saw that the poor cow really did look like the ugly Mr. Dikstra whose back curved forward like the letter S.

Then another boy pointed at the front legs of another cow and said, Look at that! Her knees are as knobby as Jenny Rozenboom's!

And look at that nose! shouted another boy. It's as big as Hilda Vander Camp's.

The boys went through the whole herd like this and the closer they looked, the more cows they found which reminded them of somebody in one way or another. Soon they could hardly look at a cow without laughing at the way it looked like some person.

When the boys sat down to milk the cows, each of them expected another to make a joke about how a cow's teats reminded them of somebody's breasts. The milk pinged against the bottoms of their empty milk pails, but nobody said anything. In a few minutes the pinging stopped as the foam took up the sound of the squirting milk. The cowbarn got very quiet, but still no one said anything. The oldest boy finished milking his cow first and got up to pour his pail of milk through the strainer into the large milk can. Then he set his pail down and watched his hands curl back into the shape of the cow's teats. He almost made a joke, but then he noticed the large teats of the next cow he would be milking. The only thing they reminded him of was the four-and-a-half gallons of white milk that would soon be passing through them.

Nothing quite like them, is there? he shouted to the other boys who did not quite understand what he had said but who kept their hands moving too so that their pails would fill with that beautiful warm milk which was the only thing any of them could think about at a time like this.

The Boys
Learn by Watching

Sometimes the farmers talked about the different ways they could tell if a sow was going to farrow. Of course everyone could see when a sow's belly was getting thick and her teats were getting full, but the trick was to be able to tell within a few hours. This way she could be penned up so that when her pigs were born there would be no danger that they would wander off and start nursing the wrong sow or that they would get stepped on by other large pigs in the hog-house.

I just watch her until she starts building her nest. Then I know she's almost due, said one farmer. Never fails.

Oh, that doesn't work, said another farmer. I've watched a sow putting mouthfuls of straw in a circle for two days and still not farrowing. The only way you can tell for sure if she's about to farrow is if she gets a little puffy in the back and starts opening.

The boys listened to the men talk like this. But they knew the men were just teasing each other. They knew the men knew the only way you could tell for sure was when the sow was lying in her nest and you would come up and rub her teats. If she was ready to farrow, she turned her belly and teats up as much as she could so that the hand that was rubbing them had an easier time of it. And if the teat hardened in the hand, and if the sow started grunting in a regular sort of beat, and if a bead of milk formed on the nipple without the hand pinching it—then you knew for sure she was going to farrow in a few hours.

The boys often hid and watched the men rubbing a sow's teats, saw how gently the palm touched and then the fingers, how the whole hand made a circle over the teat, as if the hand were shaping it. When the men left, the boys went and had their try and knew they were doing it right when the sow's low grunting sounded the same as when the men were rubbing her.

Then after they stopped rubbing, they cupped their hand the way they had over a sow's teats and stared into it the way an outfielder stares into his glove after he has caught a long fly ball. They stared into their palms proudly, as if they had put something important there, like a secret that would be there when they needed it.

Have You Ever
Seen a
Sad Sparrow?

His eye is on the sparrow
and I know He watches me.
(old gospel hymn)

The boys were bored. They walked around the farmyard.
Most of the animals were sleeping or eating. Over the fences
beyond the farmyard the corn and oats grew quietly. The
only living things that seemed busy were the sparrows. And
they were everywhere. Ruffling in the dust near the grana-
ries. Bathing in the stock tanks. Singing from the weather
vanes and cupolas.

Have you ever seen a sad sparrow? asked one of the boys.
Look at them. They act like they own everything.

Sparrows were busy building nests under barn eaves and

in willow trees. Sparrows were scavenging spilled feed from the pig troughs.

And they don't bother anybody either, said another boy. How do they do it?

The boys walked around the farmyard again, this time watching the sparrows more closely than ever. Sparrows were riding on the backs of old cows, teasing the crows by flying just over their wings, mating on the hay stacks in little bursts of feathers and dust.

The boys wandered into the grove and, still looking up at the sparrows, stumbled over some old tires. Look, said one of them. Nobody is using these old tires. Let's do something with them.

What about that old cable in the toolshed? Nobody is using that. Let's tie these tires together.

They linked a dozen old tires together with the cable. One boy climbed to the top of a cottonwood tree with a pulley, and together they hoisted the string of old tires up. They tied one end of the cable to a high branch. Now the linked tires hung down from the tree like a big necklace.

The boys used their new toy as a many-tiered swing. As a ladder. As a tree house. Or just as a comfortable place to sit and watch the rest of the world. Sometimes they got into different tires and made them weave and look like a dragon standing on its tail.

When the grown-ups got up from their naps, they agreed it was a good toy and wasn't using anything that anybody needed. In a few days sparrows built nests in the bottom curves of the tires. The nests were deep enough in the hollow spaces that they didn't bother the boys when they played on the tires. The sparrows waited until the boys were finished playing with the tires and then had their turn with them.

The
Flamethrower

The boys weren't supposed to play with matches. So when they did, they made the best of it by using them for their favorite games.

They liked to throw the match-sticks down headfirst on the sidewalk and make them pop like little firecrackers. Or they made the heads just wet enough so that they gave off a stream of smoke like rockets when the boys shot them from a BB gun. But their favorite match game was lighting each others' farts.

This was a tricky sport because it meant pulling your pants down and having someone hold a lit match very close to your bottom. The boys thought the results were worth the risk. The passed gas did not explode but did ignite like a torch with a quick blue flame.

The boys tried to see who could make the biggest flame.

They were happy that the slowest runner and the one who was poorest at baseball at least could win at this. He was a natural and didn't even have to practice at it. They called him the flamethrower, but always in a respectful voice. They knew that what he did to a match would never make the Guinness Book of Records, but at least it gave him one thing that he could do better than the rest of them.

Measles

One spring the boys all got measles and were kept in a dark room so that their eyes would not get hurt.

After a few days, when their fevers went down, the curtains were opened a little bit so that they could see. They still had to stay in bed, but it was a good time to learn how to do something new. One of them looked at a bird book and learned how to draw bird pictures. Another took up embroidery. One decided to make baskets out of grass. Another started playing music on a recorder.

Some girls from school who had already gotten over the measles came by to see the boys while they were working. They teased the boys that they were doing things that girls do.

The boys were still too sick to fight back, so they just showed what they had done. The boy who was embroidering held up a dishtowel he was working on. All the stitches were on the line and very tight. Even the French knots. Then another boy held up his pictures of ducks. They were so good the girls thought he had traced them. The grass basket another boy had made was woven so tightly that when he held it up to the light the girls could not even see a peephole. And the boy with the recorder played Yankee Doodle without missing a note.

The mothers were in the next room talking about the new vaccine for measles. Won't it be a shame, said one of the mothers, if someday boys never get sick enough to learn how to do those things?

Catching Pigeons

Somebody was buying pigeons for forty cents apiece. Why would anyone pay that much for a stupid pigeon? the grown-ups wondered. Nobody knew for sure, but somebody said something about rich Texans wanting live pigeons instead of clay ones for their skeet shoots.

The boys didn't care. Forty cents was twice what they got for a pair of pocket gopher feet, and catching pigeons would be more fun than trapping pocket gophers.

There must be twenty dollars worth in our haymow, said the oldest boy. And then there are all the neighbors' barns.

What if we run out of pigeons before we're rich? asked another boy. It was a good question, so the boys decided to leave a few pigeons here and there as breeders so they could have a regular income forever.

They found some airy gunnysacks that the pigeons

would be able to breathe through and got to work right away.

Some boys crawled along the rope that was strung across the top of the barn for pulling hay into the haymow. Just below the roof. This way they could shimmy along and trap some of the pigeons in the cupola and catch others if they landed on the rope.

The plan worked fine until the boys on the rope started catching pigeons. The idea was to throw them down to the boys who were below with the gunnysacks. But it was too far to throw pigeons. Every time one was almost in the hands of a boy below, it beat its wings and got away.

Finally, one of the boys with a gunnysack yelled, Tie the wings, then flip me the bird!

Flip you the bird? said a boy on the rope.

And that was the end of pigeon-catching. The rope jiggled with laughter. Then laughing boys fell down into the hay. Laughing boys from below climbed toward them with the gunnysacks, tried to hold a finger up to them but laughed so hard they could not raise their arms.

One laughing boy said, Think of the money, but this sounded funny.

Look! Even the pigeons are laughing, said another laughing boy, and that was funny.

In a little while all the laughing boys and laughing pigeons had laughed themselves out of the barn.

The boys never did manage to catch those pigeons. Whenever they talked about it, somebody always told the joke instead. Sometimes they thought this was just as good as having a lot of money.

Who Kept
One Hand
in Her Pocket

There was a lady who kept one hand in her pocket. When she was in the garden, weeding, one hand was hidden in her pocket. When she was feeding oats to the chickens, she scattered the grain with one hand and kept the other in her pocket. In church. In the store. Wherever she was, one hand was always in her pocket.

The boys wanted to know why this was so. They asked people, but no one else knew either. So they made a plan, a trick to make her pull her hand out. They decided to lay a string where she walked and trip her with it as she passed by. When she was falling, the hidden hand would spring from the pocket to keep her from striking her face on the ground. Then they would run out to help her get up—but really to get a look at the hand.

They started talking about what they would see. Surely

it was more than a withered hand. The lady must be hiding something better than that. A large, black pearl, one of them guessed. Or a rose carved from ruby. Or something so pretty that they would never guess what it was.

The boys laid out the string one day, but when the lady passed by, they weren't able to pull it and trip her. They got too scared thinking that if they saw what the lady had hidden, she might give it to them. And if it was as beautiful as they thought, they might have to walk around the rest of their lives with one hand in their pockets, hiding what they had discovered.

Turpentine
and Corncobs

It wasn't the boys' idea. They liked the stray dog, even if it did stink and look mean. Maybe it was growling because its paw was swollen—and maybe the paw had buckshot in it from the last farmer who saw it. The boys wanted to help the dog the way they would help any stranger who needed it. They watched the dog standing by the water supply tank with its nose like a witching stick pointing at the water pipe.

The boys had heard the men talk about a killer. Dead sheep and young calves. Little animal throats torn and little tongues eaten. Talk about wolf or coyote blood in a mad dog. The boys had heard the click of the gun chambers closing, had seen the heavy weapons leaning against the door frame.

The boys' idea was this—to water and feed that dog and put salve on its swollen foot. That's how they found out the dog was not a killer, but there was no way they could hide the dog's looks with a little food and water and black horse salve on the swollen paw. They remembered another idea they learned from the men and used it now—coaxing the dog into the tool shed where no one would hear its whimpering and snarling when they held it down and rubbed its hind end with corncobs until it bled and then splashed turpentine on the tender spot.

That's how they made sure the dog got away, howling and running to who knows where. Maybe all that pain would lead it straight back to a home it had somewhere, or at least to the river bottom with all its bushes to hide behind and all the little field mice just sitting around waiting for something to happen.

Bat Wings

On summer nights when the sun was just setting and things were starting to get boring, the men sometimes went outside with their shotguns to shoot bats. On good nights the bats circled and dived for insects over the men's heads. The men swung their guns wildly and took quick shots from the hip. But other times the bats hovered high overhead, giving the men a chance to take careful aim. That is when they found out just how good the bats' radar is, because the bats moved so quickly that the shot missed them. At those times they seemed to jump in midair, looking more like hummingbirds than bats.

The shotguns were an awfully noisy way not to get bats, and it was the boys who thought of a quieter way. Fishing for them. They took some of the grown-ups' fly rods and started casting the flies into the sky.

When the hunting isn't good, you should try fishing, said the oldest boy to the men. The men put their guns down to watch. Soon one of the boys lured a bat by casting the fly rod. The bat dived for the fly and was caught. The boy reeled the bat in from the sky while the men watched, looking surprised with their quiet guns across their knees.

Pretty soon the men tried it too and sometimes had the same good luck the boys were having.

After they caught a half dozen bats like this, they noticed that the bats never had the hook in their mouths. It was always stuck in the bats' wings.

If they have such good radar, said one of the men, why don't they catch the fly in their mouths?

Maybe their wing is just like a hand and they have to catch the fly first, said the littlest boy.

No one paid attention to the youngest boy, because his idea sounded so silly, but many years later—at thousands and thousands of dollars expense—somebody in a laboratory, using infrared cameras, found out that bats really do catch their food in their wings, using them like hands to feed themselves.

You write the moral to this story:

Hog Calls

Sometimes the boys got up very early so they could hear the first hog call of the morning. Hog calling was the farmers' way of getting each other's attention and showing who got up first. The pigs didn't have to be told when it was time to eat and usually beat even the earliest hog callers to the feeding troughs.

The boys liked to sit on top of the supply tank so they could hear in all directions. The first hog call always sounded the best. It seemed to come out of nowhere, like a falling star. It was the one that caused goose bumps and made getting up early worthwhile. It was fun to listen to the other hog calls too, but they all sounded like echoes. The farmers who were not first could just as well have gone out there and yelled, Me too! me too! And the second-comers always tried too hard. They knew they had overslept and so they tried to make up for it with weird calls. There was also the favorite joke when a farmer got up late: he'd give somebody else's hog call and try to make the neighbors think that it was somebody else who was the late-riser, but nobody was ever fooled by this. It was just part of the fun.

The grown-ups thought it was a good idea for the boys to get out there and listen to the hog calls. Listening was no way to learn how to do something yourself, but it was a good way to learn how the world worked. Sitting out there in the cold for no good reason certainly was a good start. And it was probably the knack for doing something for no good reason that would make good hog callers out of them all.

Dinner Music

The time for castrating young boars was very noisy. All the squealing and pushing by the young pigs as they tried to get away from the men who were catching them. And then the louder squealing when the testicles were being cut out.

Even though the squealing was terrible, the dog always stood by to eat the testicles as the men threw them away. When the castrating was getting started, the boys stayed away because the loud squealing got on their nerves. But they knew the dog was in the hoghouse eating testicles, and this made them so curious that after a while they would go and watch.

The dog stood next to the pen waiting for a flying testicle that the men threw to him. He did not miss. He made it look as easy as someone who is good at catching popcorn in his mouth.

Later when the castrating was over and the squealing had stopped, the boys tried to get the dog to catch dog biscuits the way he caught testicles. But the dog missed the dog biscuits most of the time.

Dinner music! shouted the oldest boy, and all the boys started squealing like pigs. The dog looked at them as if they were crazy, but he did start catching dog biscuits. It could not have been because he was hungry, but probably just to go along with the boys' game.

Head Lice

It was more than an itch, it was head lice.

Why did I get them and nobody else? asked the youngest boy. It's not fair.

But the youngest boy's troubles had just begun. Get away from us! said the older boys. Get your clothes out of our room! Don't use our combs! Don't touch our toothbrushes!

But when the youngest boy was having his head treated with tar soap, the older boys got curious. The fine-tooth comb raked the dead lice from his hair. They stacked up on the table like little vegetables from the first garden pickings. Then, after the rinsing, the work on the nits began, sliding the little white eggs off the hair between fingernails.

I see one, one of the older boys said, and reached for the hair to pull the nit off between his fingernails.

There's another one, said another boy.

Getting all the nits was a big job, so one of the grown-ups made popcorn while the boys worked on the nits. They would have a little celebration when the work was done. The boys made the work more interesting by counting to see who could pick the most nits. Now, instead of crawling with lice, the youngest boy's head was crawling with hands. And everybody was talking at once. His hair was like a field of oats in July filled with busy harvesters.

The Throw-up Pan

One winter the boys all got the flu at the same time. The headaches and fever and nausea were bad enough, but the worst thing was that there was only one throw-up pan to go around. During the day this was no problem—they just put it in the middle of the room and whoever needed it could walk or crawl over to it. But at night in the dark was different—someone might wake up needing it right away and not be able to find it in time.

So the boys fought over who got to sleep with the throw-up pan next to his pillow. When they drew straws for it, somebody would always wait until the others were asleep and then sneak over and get it to put by his own pillow.

The oldest boy had an idea. Since it was a metal pan, they could punch little holes in the rim. This way each boy could tie a string to it. The throw-up pan could stay in the middle of the room and each boy could have the end of his string next to his pillow to pull if he needed the throw-up pan in a hurry.

This method worked well. Most of the boys tied their favorite toy to their end of the string so it would be easy to find in the dark. But the littlest boy tied his string to a loose tooth. He figured this way it would be easy to find his string if he needed the pan, and if someone else needed it he would get rid of the loose tooth while asleep. Since the older boys no longer had baby teeth, they could not use the littlest boy's clever idea, but they still praised him for his invention. It was one of those good ideas that can make everyone feel better during a bad time.

The
Inside Rats

During the day, when the boys saw a rat near the corncrib or barn or eating from a pig trough, it was as if a match were struck inside them. They dropped whatever toys they were playing with and ran for pitchforks or sticks to kill the rat.

But at night the boys sometimes lay awake listening to rats run through the attic and walls. The ones that made it that far up in the house were usually lost and ran wildly back and forth trying to find a way out. The boys knew that at one place near the ceiling was a hole. When a lost rat ran over that spot, it fell between the wall studs down to the floor, right there in their room with nothing but the thin wall separating them. Then the boys had the fun of hearing the rat scramble around trying to climb back up the plaster boards. When they put their hands on the wall, they could feel the rat's claws scratching on the other side. They could feel how far up the wall the rat was, and when they slapped that spot, the rat fell to the floor to try again.

Sometimes the boys did not slap the spot. Instead, they put their palms on the wall where the rat was scratching. The rat's claws tickled their fingertips and they scratched back, tickling the rat's paws. The rat seemed to like this and calmed down when the boys scratched the wall. Soon it climbed the wall slowly and walked quietly through the attic back to wherever it came from. And the boys went back where they came from—into their beds—much calmer too.

Winter Chores

On freezing winter nights the boys had two chores before
going to sleep. They had to tie the blankets down to the
bedframes so that they would not toss their covers off in
their dreams and freeze their hands and feet. And they had
to empty the chamber pot so that what was in it would not
freeze and need thawing out on the stove in the morning.

One night they remembered to tie down the blankets but
forgot to empty the pot. When they were all settled in,
someone remembered the pot, but it was so cold that night
that no one would get out of bed to take it out. Storm windows had already been put on so they could not even cheat
by emptying it out the window.

They argued for a while about whose turn it was to empty
the pot and then argued about who would have to thaw it
out in the morning if nobody emptied it that night.

If we keep arguing like this, it is going to freeze before we even go to sleep, said one boy.

At least arguing is making it nice and warm under the covers, said another.

That gave the littlest boy an idea. Let's keep the pot under the blankets with us tonight—then it won't freeze, he said.

It will have to be in your bed, said the oldest boy.

All right, said the youngest, if you will be the one who gets out of bed to get it.

The oldest boy jumped out of bed and ran across the cold linoleum floor to get it.

The littlest boy had to loosen his blankets a little bit to get the pot in with him. He put it right under his feet so that he would not tip it. At first, the metal pot felt cold, but soon it warmed up with him and seemed to keep his feet warm. He told the other boys about this and within a few nights all the boys were willing to take their turn with the pot in bed with them. Sometimes they even fought over who could have it in his bed—but not so much that they spilled any of it.

Big Bull

He was an ordinary Hereford calf when he was born. But friendlier and more playful than most. The boys liked him right away and spent more time brushing and playing with him than with the other calves.

When the boys walked into the barn, Little Bull ran up and put his wet nose to their faces and tried to lick their ears. The boys tickled and wrestled him until he was tired of playing. Then they rubbed his white head and fed him from their hands. He grew very fast. Soon he was big enough to go out into the cattle yard where the boys rode him bareback from one fence to another. But one day, after Little Bull had playfully thrown one of the boys off his back, he turned with his head down and pawed the dirt. Maybe Little Bull was still playing. Maybe he was getting mean. That was the day the boys changed Little Bull's name to Bull.

The boys knew the men would sell Bull if they thought he was getting mean. They made sure Bull would stay tame by making a mixture of cracked corn and molasses. Any time he got a little bit wild, the boys brought the bucket. That good feed always made him happy and friendly.

But it also made him bigger. Much bigger. Soon he was big enough to breed cows, and the men talked about what a fine bull he was. They figured calves from this fine big bull would be hearty, friendly, and strong. The boys kept playing with him, and feeding him to keep him tame. He only walked when they rode him bareback, but he still liked the attention. It was not long before Bull was fat. When he got his forefeet up on a cow, her back bent like a cherry tree limb with too many boys on the sack swing. The time came when he was so fat that he could hardly get his chin up on a cow's back, let alone his forelegs. He wagged his tail when the boys approached, but he didn't seem to be able to show his affection in any other way.

That's when the men said, We'll have to sell him. He's so fat he's useless as tits on a boar.

But this is not the end of the story for Big Bull. When the stock truck came to get him, he was too big to fit through the chute onto the truck.

The boys thought they and Big Bull might be lucky after all, but the men were very clever that day and thought of a way to put a hay sling around Big Bull's stomach to hoist him enough for the truck to drive under. The hay sling was just three heavy strands of rope that came together to a ring on each end, like a hammock. Hay was stacked on the sling, and a rope came down from the hoisting beam which stuck out from the top of the barn over the big hay door. Horses pulled big loads of hay up into the haymow like this:

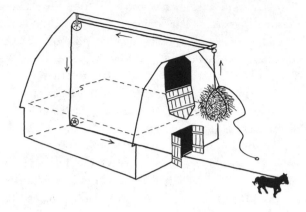

The men had the boys lead Big Bull out to the barn with their bucket of cracked corn and molasses. But what the men did not know was that when the ropes tightened on Big Bull's stomach he would let out a very loud bellow. Which scared the horses. And sent them on a runaway. Which sent Big Bull shooting forty feet straight up like a big yo-yo on a string. The men got the horses stopped, but only after Big Bull was dangling in the middle of the barn, thirty feet above the haymow floor. There was no way to pull Big Bull back out of the barn since the only rope attached to the hay sling was the trip-rope. The men backed the horses up, easing Big Bull down into the haymow. The only way out now was through the little openings in the haymow floor at the tops of the ladders that people used to climb up there.

The truck driver went home, promising to tell no one about this. The men closed the big hay door and put the horses away. The boys brought Big Bull a bucket of cracked corn and molasses to make him feel good. In a few minutes everything looked normal. From the outside.

Don't tell anyone about this, said one of the men. We'll

butcher him up there and nobody will ever have to know about this.

But one of the boys said, Why don't we just tell people that Big Bull climbed up the haymow?

At first the men said no, but then they looked at each other and laughed. And laughed some more when they thought of the looks on people's faces if they saw Big Bull in the haymow.

So the men and boys went into town to the sale barn where everyone was standing around talking. You know that big bull we got? Well, that critter clumb right up the haymow.

Of course, no one believed this story. Then the men started taking bets, and that got people coming over in a hurry to look. The boys pulled out some of Big Bull's hair and stuck it to the boards at the top of one of the ladders going up the haymow to make it look as if that was the opening Big Bull squeezed through. And they loosened a couple of the ladder rungs to make it look as if the ladder almost gave way on him as he climbed up.

In a few days people were coming from all over the county to see that big bull that climbed up the haymow. Some families brought picnic lunches and made the visit into an outing.

Big Bull just sat there calmly in the middle of the haymow. He didn't move much but he looked happier than ever with all of this attention—with all those people coming to feed and pet and admire him. And it is no wonder. He always was a friendly one.

Bidding

Oopie Feikes was the cleverest bidder at the sale barn. For years only the auctioneer and the man in the ring knew how he signalled a bid.

Sometimes half the men in the sale barn watched Oopie when cattle came into the ring that they thought he might buy. Does he bid by touching his cap? By lifting his thumb—the only finger on that hand he had not lost in the cornpicker? Or does he just frown a certain way? It was no use. No one could tell how he bid, and so no one could have the fun of bidding him up on something he wanted very much.

Oopie was a skinny, jittery fellow who was usually very busy with his hands, feet, lips, and eyes. Many people thought that was his secret—that he was hiding his bid somewhere in all his jitteriness. In fact, when he did take a bid, it seemed harder than ever to see that he had done any-thing unusual.

It was a boy who finally said, He doesn't do anything when he bids. At first the men ignored the boy's remark, but then they noticed it too—the only time Oopie wasn't doing something was when he took a bid. After a while, as the word got around, everyone could tell what the auction-eer and the man in the ring could tell all those years—and that was that when Oopie wanted a cow or calf or ring full of steers bad enough, all the busyness of his body stopped and he sort of sat still glowing with desire. That was his way of bidding. Some people out there learned something from that, and would watch other people closely even when they did not seem to be doing anything. Often what they wanted started to show all over them.

Groundhog
Day

The boys were out to see if the groundhog could see his shadow. They could see their own shadows, but what if the groundhog was standing in the shade when he looked for his? Since they wanted to be the first to know what was going to happen with the weather, they wanted to be sure to see what the groundhog saw when he looked for his shadow.

They knew where a groundhog hole was, so they found a good place to sit in the grass and watch for it.

The sun came out and then a cloud came over. The sun again and clouds for a while. But no groundhog. The boys stayed out there all day watching, sending one boy to run for food when they needed it. The sun started to set and soon shadows would be everywhere.

Look! said one boy. Wasn't that the groundhog?

Where? said another.

Yes, there! said another, but he was pointing to a different spot.

The groundhog was everywhere and nowhere.

Looks like the groundhog changes as much as the weather around here, said one of the boys. The boys were not sure if they knew any more than anyone else about the weather after sitting out there all day. But as they walked toward the house, the air felt strange. Not really warm, not really cold. One of those evenings when you cannot tell if it is winter or spring.

Some Theories
on Rat Tails

One thing the boys noticed about cats and rats was that when a cat ate a rat, it always left the tail.

The question was, Why don't cats eat the rats' tails?

I know! said one boy. They leave it for the rat-tail fairy who puts a bowl of milk there for it!

No, stupid, said the oldest boy. Then you'd find bowls of milk instead of rat tails!

I know, said another boy. They leave it there so it will grow back another rat for them to eat!

No, stupid, said the oldest boy. Then you'd see all these rat tails with only half-grown rats back on them!

I know, said the littlest boy. The cats use the rat tails for tooth picks.

The oldest boy couldn't think of any reason why this

might not be so. But he still said, Have you ever seen a cat pick its teeth with a rat's tail?

No, said the littlest boy, but have you ever seen a cat with dirty teeth?

The boys went out and checked some cats' teeth. They were clean.

I always knew toothbrushes were humbug, said the oldest boy, having the last word on the matter.

Butterflies

When the men were out working in the fields, it was easy to tell them apart. Even if you could not see their faces or if you were not close enough to make out their size and shape, the way they moved was enough to show who they were. If one bent over to pull a thistle or leaned his elbow on a fence post, it was as if he were writing his name on the air in big red letters—it was so clear who he was.

But on Sundays when the men were dressed in dark suits and sitting in the church pews, they looked alike. All those suntanned faces up to the white forehead where the hat band started. And during congregational prayer when they bowed their heads together, they seemed to turn into plants that had budded in a field of straight rows. The only way you could tell who was who was by remembering where each one always sat.

But when the worshipping was over and they walked out of the rose-windowed church, they were like butterflies coming out of cocoons. All their different colors got brighter and clearer as they went back into the sun toward the sparkling fields. And one by one in their own ways they became themselves again.

Spontaneous Combustion

One night a neighbor's barn caught fire. Hay that had been put up in the haymow too wet burst into flames in the middle of the night. The farmer woke up when the light of the burning barn shone in his eyes. It was like a dawn that had come too early. And from the wrong direction.

Fire trucks came from four different towns. All of those sirens woke the neighborhood. Everyone dressed quickly and followed the fire trucks and the light of the burning barn. They parked their cars along the road and in the fields near the fire, then ran out to make a big circle around the barn and the fire trucks.

The barn did not have a chance. The roof was burning and the framework glowed through the flames like a neon skeleton. People stood watching and saying, What a shame, and What a pity. But the owner was screaming and pointing at the corner of the barn. My pigs! he shouted. They're still in there!

Now the crowd could hear the squealing pigs and the noise of their scuffling bodies against the barn wall. No one talked anymore and a few started walking back to their cars. A young fireman ran toward the barn with an ax. Other firemen turned hoses on him so that he had a suit of splashing water. He chopped at the barn and right away a pig snout came through. Now the squealing was louder than ever, but the fireman chopped again and ran back toward the fire trucks. The siding splintered and a large black sow came out followed by a stream of pigs. All sizes and colors. Ten. Twenty. Fifty pigs. The firemen turned the hoses on them. The pigs sizzled and steamed when the water hit them. They stood still and let the firemen spray them. In a few minutes they ran into the crowd.

At first people did not seem to believe it. The pigs were all right. Someone reached over and rubbed ashes from the singed bristles of one pig. Then everyone was reaching for the pigs and petting them. People started laughing and joking. The whole crowd burst out in celebration. It could have been the Fourth of July or the end of a war, the way they were acting. Somebody had some popcorn and somebody else had some apples and coffee. They gave some to the owner first and then passed around what they had. A case of beer came out of somebody's trunk. A watermelon and three cantaloupes came from somewhere. And the pigs were part of it all, coming right up to people and eating from their hands. Where are the marshmallows? somebody asked, but no one was interested in the fire anymore. It was one big ball of flames and was not going to do anything but burn itself out. The firemen gave up on it too and started to have fun with the pigs and other people. They pointed their hoses up. The spray came down on the happy crowd of people and pigs. And that was probably the first time ever that anyone saw a rainbow made by water from fire hoses and the light of a burning barn.

Part II

Who Made
Her Husband Do
All the Work

There was a woman down the road who made her husband do all the work. Not just the chores and fieldwork but the housework too. When he finished milking the cows, she might help him carry the milk in, but only so that he would get to the house a little sooner to cook supper. On Monday mornings she got up early to make coffee, but only so that he would awaken in time to do the wash before going out to feed the pigs. If she was busy, you could be sure it was only to make him busier. Most of the time she sat in her rocking chair next to the kitchen window looking out to see that he was doing the work she had told him to do.

In time, the husband came to be very lean and haggard while the wife was plump and cheerful. Some people said she was just plain working him to death. But these were not the people who knew the rest of the story. The part that started every night when this woman sent her husband out to a small shed in the grove to wash eggs. He would shuffle out there after his long day's work, hang up a lantern, and sit down under it on his small stool. In a half-circle around the stool he had several buckets of eggs that he had gathered during the day. Now he hummed to himself as he carefully washed each egg with a wet dishcloth and placed it in the large egg crate.

Soon people came from all over the neighborhood. Because when they did, this lean and tired man would tell stories as nobody could tell stories. Within an hour after the lantern was lit, the little shed was packed with men, women, and children listening to one story after another.

The one about the chicken with three legs! someone would shout, or How about the one about the woman who wouldn't cut her fingernails? He'd tell them their favorite stories and then, every night, add one or two new ones. Sometimes people would try to help him wash eggs as he was talking, but he would never let them. He knew just how long he wanted the stories and egg-washing to take. And everyone knew that the last story was about to end when he was washing the last egg.

While he was telling stories, his wife was in her rocking chair where she could watch the people coming from all over the neighborhood. She always had her note pad on her lap where she could write down all the work she had planned for her husband the next day. Now and then she smiled as she looked out toward the shed, as if what was happening there was part of her plan too.

Scar Tissue

He stopped chewing on his cigar and laid it down next to the lantern. It simmered there on the burnt spot where he had laid other cigars. He picked out an egg from the bucket and rubbed at a spot with the damp dishcloth. He would start talking now. The boys sat at the edge of the hoop of lantern light and looked up at his face.

Well, I'm a pretty old farmer, he said. I can remember the days before rat poison. There was as many rats back then as good stories. Good talkers and good workers. In those days you could tell the speed of a man's hands by checking the scar tissue on his legs.

He held an egg up to the lantern light, as if he could tell this way which ones would be culled out at the hatchery.

One time we was shelling corn. Corn shelling. Five or six of us shoving corn in the hopper. We was going for a thousand bushels. Big crib. And big rats. I don't know how many. Lots of them. They was legion. We seen their tails slickering in the corn. They was digging right ahead of our scoops.

He laid an egg down and wiggled his short forefinger as if he could make it look like a rat's tail. He picked up his cigar, chewed on it, and laid it down on the burnt spot again.

First thing you gotta know about rats is they're dumb, but they know when they're in trouble. The second thing you gotta know is that when they're in trouble, they don't run for light—they run for dark.

He adjusted the wick on the lantern. The egg bucket was not quite half empty. The boys leaned back on their hands.

So we was almost to the bottom of this corn when we run into them rats. First one trickles out. Then the whole works. Like when one ear of corn falls out of the pile and then it all comes down. So we start stomping. I must of stomped a dozen of them when the fella next to me misses one when he stomps. And that rat swickers around real quick and comes at me from the side where I can't see him. He is looking for a dark tunnel. And he finds it. My pants leg! He saw that little tunnel over my shoe and up he comes. I had on wool socks, the thick kind that gives rat claws something good to dig into. Good footing. So he gets his claws in my wool socks, looks up the tunnel, and don't see daylight. He must of thought he was home free for sure.

He paused and rubbed his chin while the boys squirmed.

Well, you know, in those days, rats was always running up somebody's leg. Specially during corn shelling. I guess it was just my turn. You just had to figure on it a little bit during corn shelling. Like getting stung when you're going after honey. You was always hearing somebody yelling and seeing him kick his leg like crazy in a corncrib or pulling his pants off so fast you'd think he got the instant diarrhea.

Now let me show you the scar that critter give me.

He pulled up his overalls. His leg was white and hairless. Just below the knee, on the inside calf, was a set of jagged scars.

That's how fast my hands was, he said. I grabbed that sucker before he could clear my shoestrings. He rubbed the scars with the tip of his finger, gently, as if they were still tender.

There's the top teeth. And there's the bottom, he said. I grabbed and I squeezed. And I squeezed. And the rat bites. And he bites. I felt his rib cage crack, but his teeth stayed in me like they was hog rings. I guess we both got our way. Now he's still hanging there dead inside my pants while we killed the rest of them rats. Then I pried him loose with my pocketknife. Stubborn sucker. But he knew a dark tunnel when he seen one.

There were only two eggs left in the bucket. He rinsed the washcloth and took one more chew on his cigar. He picked up an egg and rolled it over in his hand looking for spots.

Now almost any old farmer can tell you his rat story. They've all had a rat or two up their pants. But just ask him to show you his scar tissue. I can wager you this—the ones with slow hands won't show you where they got theirs.

The boys giggled a little as he put the last egg into the crate with his careful hands. It was time to make their escape. The door to the shed was open.

Watch out for the dark now, he said as the boys filed out, their shirttails fluttering behind them into the night.

You Know
What Is Right

Before the boys went into town on Saturday nights, the grown-ups always warned them to stay out of trouble by saying, You know what is right. Always those words: *You know what is right.* After hearing the same warning over and over many times, the boys figured they really must know what is right. But when they were on the downtown streets, it was not always so easy.

One Saturday night the first thing that happened was some town boys gave them the finger and yelled,

Hey, Stinkeroos,
You got cowshit on your shoes!

The oldest boy answered quickly by giving them the finger too and yelling,

Oh yeah, city fellow?
Your underpants is yellow!

The youngest boy said, Yelling at them like that, was that right?

The other boys were not sure. They walked away from the town boys thinking about it. Was that right? Was that right? they said over and over to themselves. A little later they stopped in front of a new car show window. They leaned against the glass and looked up and down the streets, wondering what might happen next.

Stop leaning against that window! shouted the sales manager. The boys knew the man could tell by their work shoes and overalls that they were from the farm. Inside, the man was showing new cars to a well-dressed couple who looked as if they must be town folks. Let's do a stinkeroo, said the oldest boy.

The boys made their plan. They got into the next car that the well-dressed couple would be looking at. The boys who could passed gas. Then they all slipped out and closed the car doors behind them. They watched from across the street as the couple got into the stinky car. The man looked at the woman and said something. Then the woman spoke to the man with an angry look on her face. They were blaming each other for the smell, all right. Then they got out and looked at the sales manager as if maybe he were the one who made the car stink. They shook their heads and left.

The boys tried not to laugh in front of the couple, but then the youngest boy said, But was that right?

This made one boy laugh aloud, and soon they were running down the street laughing loudly. Stop! said one of the boys. I'm going to wet my pants!

But would that be right? asked another. Now they all laughed so hard that they were all afraid of wetting their pants.

The gas station john! one of them shouted. They ran

74 *You Know What Is Right*

toward it to relieve themselves. The oldest boy was the first
one to the urinal.

Inside the urinal was a handful of change. It was the kind
of urinal that has a few inches of water in the bottom, like a
cup. Someone had dropped the change into the urinal and
then urinated on it. If anyone flushed the urinal, the change
would go too. But for anyone to get the change he would
have to stick his hand into someone else's urine.

The boys looked at each other, and it was as if for the first
time that night a clear light went on in their minds.

The oldest boy reached into his pocket for some change,
dropped it into the urinal, then stepped closer and urinated
over the raised ante.

Me too, said the next boy, stepping up politely. And so,
in turn, each gave his share of money and urine until the
mound of coins glowed like a collection plate.

Now *that* was the right thing to do, said the last boy as he
buttoned up.

Who Grew
Snakes
in Her Orchard

Down the road lived an old woman who grew snakes in her orchard, then paid the boys to kill them. The boys got very good at this job, catching the snakes with sticks that had forked nails on the end. They slipped these down over the snake heads and picked them up unhurt.

The old woman wanted to see them alive before she would talk money. So the boys brought them to her in plastic sacks, and she would look in to see the squirming garters blaming each other for their misery. She got a little puffy when she saw them, but she would bring money. Ten cents apiece.

The boys took out one snake at a time so she could count them. They hit the snake heads with rocks, right there on her sidewalk where she would see it all. When they finished, the old woman paid them, and they put the bloody snakes back in the sacks.

When the boys were out of view of the old woman's house, they emptied the sacks on the ground. Most snakes still squirmed a little, but the boys could tell, after doing this many times, which ones would live past sunset. They took the live ones home and put them in the cellar. The next morning they fed these survivors vegetables and milk, then carried them out to the pasture where they would not be able to find their way back to the old woman's orchard. The boys figured it would be unfair to the snakes and to the old woman if they killed the same snake twice.

Who Saw
the Prickly Pear

When Marta was fifteen years old, she started growing whiskers. Not just a hair here and there on her chin, and not the kind of soft little moustache some boys think is pretty on a girl. No, Marta grew a beard that was so thick that she came to school with razor scrapes from trying to get a clean shave. By late afternoon her whiskers were perking up in a dark brown stubble that everyone could see.

In other ways Marta was delicate. Her voice was soft, her arms and body were thin, and when she walked she was like a feather carried by a gentle breeze. When a strange boy came to the neighborhood, he seemed always to be drawn toward Marta more than the other girls. But when a boy came close enough to talk to her, he'd see her bristly whiskers. In a few minutes he'd find an excuse to slip away.

It's awful, said one boy soon after he had met Marta at a

basketball game, I thought I was in love. Then I saw the prickly pear.

Nobody likes a girl with whiskers, said his friend who was older and always seemed to talk wisely.

But then, from her place in the bleachers, Marta looked down at them in her slender and glowing way.

I think I am in love again, said the boy who could no longer see her whiskers. Before his older friend could speak, he put his own bristly chin into his palm and, rubbing hard, took stock of what he knew and began to teach his hand to like what it felt.

The Old
Policeman

One Saturday night when the boys went into town, they found a basement window of the church open. They gathered a basket of ripe tomatoes out of people's gardens, climbed into the church, went through the sanctuary, and up into the church steeple. From here they could throw ripe tomatoes at passing cars.

They hid behind the brick bulwarks at the base of the cone. The steeple cone reached twenty feet above them to the cross on the pinnacle and over a hundred feet over the street below them.

They were situated like this:

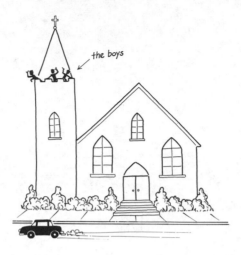

the boys

They missed the first few cars that passed, the tomatoes landing on the street behind them. Then they found their mark and tomatoes splattered over windshields and hoods and cartops and trunks. A few minutes later the police car came speeding to the scene. The boys didn't realize how safe they felt until they found themselves lobbing tomatoes at the police car. One tomato landed on the hood, another on the red flasher.

Bull's-eye, said one of the boys.

The policeman stopped, turned on the flasher, and shone his spotlight on the bushes across the street. Look, said one of the boys. It's the old policeman.

There was some comfort in this. The old policeman was kind. And he was so slow that he never seemed to catch anyone. But he was very good with the spotlight and had a reputation for doing with the spotlight what he couldn't do with his legs.

Seeing that it was the old policeman, the boys were not

afraid. One of them threw another tomato. No, the other boys warned in a loud whisper.

It was another hit. Now the police car made a quick U-turn and the spotlight started running around under the bushes near the church like a coon dog with a hot scent. Then the spotlight made a few quick leaps up the church steps. The boys crouched behind the bulwarks. The spotlight jumped a few times, as if it were sniffing the air, and then ran straight up the side of the steeple. It hopped over the heads of the boys without touching them and all the way to the pinnacle above them.

The spotlight sat quietly on the pinnacle and illuminated the cross while the boys breathed heavy. They lay on their backs staring at the glowing crucifix. Then suddenly the light was gone and the boys heard the police car drive away.

Soon the boys were safely out of the church and back downtown. The police car was parked on the corner where it usually was when the old policeman was on duty. He had wiped the police car clean from the splattered tomatoes and was leaning against it. Now and then he stopped boys who passed by and checked their palms for evidence. But something in the boys told them that the old policeman knew. And that he had already had his say.

The Coyotes
Are Coming Back

There weren't supposed to be any coyotes out there any more. The last ones had been killed with cyanide traps almost twenty years ago. Coyotes? Not out here. We know how to take care of coyotes. The ones that walk on two legs and the ones that walk on four.

But there was howling in the night. Just a little bit. As if a coyote had wandered out there to test the air. Did you hear a coyote last night? A few people did. The rest laughed. Then some people started making coyote sounds at night to make fun of the ones who heard the real coyote sounds. Soon the idea of a coyote out there was a joke nobody took seriously.

Except the boys. They went out to find the coyote. And not only did they find pheasant feathers that a coyote had left—they found coyote hair on the barbed-wire fence! A few gray hairs. The boys knew they were not from any animal they usually saw around there. But where was the coyote now?

The boys walked the line fences where the grass was knee high. Not there. They walked along the railroad track where there were small willows and rose bushes to hide under. Not there. They walked along the creek bed. Not there. They looked down the corn rows and in the alfalfa fields. Not there. They climbed the windmill where they could see for miles in all directions. No coyote. In all their looking they hadn't even seen a coyote track. All they had were some pheasant feathers and a few gray hairs. They knew they wouldn't be able to prove anything with these. They threw the feathers away but kept the coyote hairs in a small jar where they could look at them whenever they wanted to. They took turns sliding the coyote hairs between their fingers and trying to guess what a whole coyote would look like.

The boys figured the coyote was being shy and hiding so well because it didn't trust anybody in its new neighborhood. They decided to change that. They found a dead chicken and brought it to the spot where they had found the pheasant feathers. The next morning there were nothing but chicken feathers. They brought out a dish of milk and a dead rat. The next morning these were gone. Then they brought a pork chop and some strawberries. And as they were leaving, they saw the coyote. Standing in the alfalfa field watching them. It didn't run. It just stood there as if it knew they were the ones who were bringing food every day.

Wow! Look at him! Look at those ears! Look at those legs!

The boys had never seen a wild animal that big in the fields out there before and stood watching it while it watched them.

Now what do we do? said one of the boys.

I suppose we had better tell the grown-ups so they can set cyanide traps, said the oldest boy.

Spitting Sally

One day the boys went to visit their cousin in town. They went with him to the town park where many town boys were playing. Some were rolling marbles near the band shelter, some were sliding backwards down the high slide, and many were playing softball on the park diamond. But the boys were most interested in what was happening close to the horseshoe stakes. A girl about ten years old stood with her back towards a group of town boys who were throwing stones at her.

What's going on here? one of the boys asked.

Oh, that's Spitting Sally, said their cousin. She's real stupid. Flunked third grade three times. She always comes out here by the horseshoe stakes so kids can throw stones at her.

The boys walked closer to the girl. She had on a furry

hooded coat and did not seem to be getting hurt when stones hit her.

Let's help her, said the oldest farm boy, who then picked up a stone and threw it at the town boys.

I wouldn't do that if I were you, said their cousin.

But another one of the boys already had picked up a stone too and threw it at the town boys. You mean bastards! he yelled as he threw.

But while the boys were watching to see if their stones found their mark, Spitting Sally spat. A slimy mouthful of pink spit that smelled like pink peppermints. She hit both boys in their faces.

I warned you, said their cousin. If you don't know the game, you shouldn't try to play.

The town boys threw another volley of stones. Spitting Sally turned her furry back and through her wet pink lips giggled like someone at her own birthday party.

Who Didn't
Want
an Indoor Toilet

When times got good, everybody got indoor toilets. Most people kept the outdoor privy too for when the weather was nice or for when their feet were too muddy to come in the house. You had to be a pretty bad farmer not to be able to afford an indoor toilet.

Except one rich farmer. He didn't want an indoor toilet.

When other farmers asked him why he didn't have one, he told them things like this.

Houses are places where you go to have good times with your family. To eat. To sleep. To play with your children. To make children. Now you people with your indoor toilets, what have you done to your houses? You put a place for people to shit in them and call it improvement! Think of this—somebody says, I have to go to the toilet, and instead of going outside they just go into the next room. Now how are the rest of you supposed to feel when you know that person is right on the other side of that door—only a few feet away—shitting! At least people with chamber pots could hide them behind the bed. But your indoor toilet is always there. Pretty soon your kitchen smells like shit. And you call that modern! You call that civilized! A house is almost a holy place. Now you tell me what kind of person would build a room for shitting in a place like that! Not even a dog shits in his own house.

Nobody could argue with him really. They just tried not to talk about toilets with him. Because when they did they couldn't help feeling a little bit foolish for what they had done to themselves and their houses.

Corncobs
and
Peach Tissues

During the summer the boys had to use the outhouse. It was a rule. No sense using all that water for flushing and no sense tracking up the house when the weather is nice enough to use the outhouse.

The boys didn't mind using the outhouse. Except for the corncobs. After a while the corncobs didn't bother them, but the boys were always glad when peaches arrived at the grocery stores in town. They didn't like peaches very much, but they liked the soft tissue paper that peaches were packed in. When the peaches were unpacked, the soft paper was put in the outhouse and could be used instead of corncobs.

When the peach tissues were used up, it was back to corncobs. Just when the boys were getting used to the soft tissues! For a few weeks their tender skin got sore from the corncobs. But then they would get used to scratchy cobs and weren't bothered by them very much.

The corncobs and tissues taught the boys a few lessons. They learned that having things bad is not so bad so long as you don't know how good things can be. But having things good after having things bad is even better than having things good when they've been good all the time. And even though having things bad after having them good is worse than not knowing how good things can be, it's still better to have some good with the bad than not to have any good at all. Even so, it isn't exactly six of one and half dozen of the other. There are more corncobs than peach tissues in the world, that is for sure.

The Hootchie
Kootchie

It was safe for the boys to go into the hootchie-kootchie tent after dark because by that time all the old ladies at the fair had gone home and were not watching to see if the managers of the show were checking ID's. The boys slipped in line and laid their dollars down without any questions.

After a few card-trick acts and some monkeys riding unicycles, the boys wondered if it was worth the dollar. But then the women came on with fast music playing over the loudspeakers. This was it, all right—high-heeled shoes that glittered silver and brassieres that glittered silver. The women carried long black feathery streamers that they made dance on the air.

They're as good with those feathery things as cowboys are with a lasso, said one of the boys.

In a few minutes the women threw the streamers through

the air and acted as if they were going to take off all their clothes. But they only took off their loose skirts and went on dancing in tight shorts that glittered silver. When the dance was over, the announcer said, And now those of you who want to see the *real* show can join us in our limited viewing area in the back of the tent. Admission is two dollars.

Some people booed and walked out, but the boys had heard about this and had their money ready.

Into the rear of the tent they went, and there was another, smaller stage. Some soldiers in uniform got the best seats up close, but the boys still had a clear view.

When everyone who had paid the extra two dollars was seated, the announcer introduced a middle-aged woman named Sensational Susie. The music started and Susie took off all her clothes as quickly as someone getting ready for a bath.

The soldiers led the applause and the boys clapped too. Susie lit a cigarette, squatted, and put the lit cigarette between her legs. With her vagina she took a puff. Everyone applauded. Then she blew the smoke in a soldier's face.

Now that's Sensational *Sucking* Susie! shouted the announcer. What do you think of that?

The crowd roared.

Susie turned her back to the audience and put the cigarette between her buttocks. This time she took a puff through her anus and blew the smoke in another soldier's face.

The applause almost lifted the tent off its stakes, and the boys could imagine people outside who heard and wished now they had paid the extra two dollars.

Then the announcer said, How about getting one of those young boys back there to come forward?

The boys turned around, but there was no one younger behind them.

No, not behind you. You! shouted the announcer. Everyone looked at the boys. One of you come forward and hold a cigarette for Susie to take out of your mouth in her unusual way.

We don't smoke! shouted the oldest boy bravely.

Well, then, what do you do? Do you drink beer?

Sometimes, said the oldest boy.

The announcer had them this time. Susie took an unfinished beer bottle from one of the soldiers, held it between her legs and pretended to, or really did, urinate in it.

Give those boys some of this home brew! shouted the announcer. The soldiers cheered and passed the bottle back toward the boys, but before it got to them, one of the soldiers poured it over another's head and the crowd laughed and cheered.

The announcer calmed the crowd down and announced Susie's last number.

Trumpets blared over the loudspeakers, then snare drums. Susie with her legs set like a weight-lifter's and her arms akimbo, started swaying from side to side so that her breasts swung from side to side. The music became a marching song and as Susie slowed the motion of her shoulders, the breasts kept swaying, faster and faster, until they were rotating. But in opposite directions! Synchronized somehow not to collide over her breastbone!

Propelled at great speed, the breasts drew the loudest applause of the evening. At the peak of the speed and applause, one of the breasts came loose and went flying through the air. The announcer and Susie had this act down well. The breast flew through the air like a wobbly football right into the announcer's arms.

How about this! he shouted, bobbing the breast like a water balloon.

Susie stood there with her one real breast still rotating,

but much slower now. The boys could see, between rotations, the scar where her other breast had been removed and the little skin-like plastic hooks that held the fake breast in place. She looked past the soldiers and straight at the boys, her eyes glaring and her lips frozen in a cold grin.

The boys slipped out quickly through the side of the tent as the others applauded Susie's last act. The midway was still busy and they figured no one saw them leave the tent.

They stopped near a booth where people tossed coins into dishes. If the coin stayed in the dish, the tosser got the dish. There were several girls tossing coins and giggling and nudging each other as they kept losing nickels. The girls did not notice the boys who stood watching quietly. In a few minutes, the oldest boy said, Let's go. Those girls looked so pretty to him that he knew if they kept watching he would cry right there in front of a whole midway full of people out looking for laughs.

The Bad Day

One day everything went wrong.

Look at that pigeon! shouted one of the boys.

It was staggering near a pig feeding trough, touching one wing tip to the ground to keep from falling on its side.

Maybe it's the heat, said the oldest boy, and they ran to the sick pigeon and caught it. It gagged as if it were going to vomit. Its eyes were glazed, and one eyelid did not open again after it blinked.

Quick, the tank! the oldest boy shouted. They ran to the water tank with the dying pigeon, held its head back, and splashed handfuls of water into its open beak.

The water made the pigeon gag even more, but out came a large kernel of corn. Coughing up the kernel was like turning a switch on inside the pigeon, which panted and started beating its wings. In a few seconds it flew off, full of life.

That was stupid, said a grown-up who had been watching from the hog house. Don't you know pigeons are the one bird that drinks with its head down? You could have drowned it with its head tilted back like that.

The boys were going to explain, but they saw that the man was having a bad day. A sow had accidentally lain on another of its piglets, leaving only four from the litter of ten. The man picked up the limp body of the last victim and flung it through the air onto the manure pile.

Another dead one, he said.

But when the piglet hit the manure pile, out came a grunting sound.

Hey! shouted one of the boys, but the man had already heard it and had run over to the piglet. He held its snout in his hand and blew into its nostrils, then lay it on his knee and patted its small rib cage. The steady tapping was so much like applause that the boys clapped their hands. In a few seconds the piglet squealed and struggled to get away.

I wonder if that will teach you to get out of the way next time, scolded the man as he put the piglet back in the pen with its mother.

What a bad day, the man said. He kicked a pig trough to show what a bad mood he was in. A mouse that had been stuck under the trough scurried away with its tail bleeding.

Well, at least the cats have it good, said one of the boys, trying to cheer the man up. They looked at the four cats that were sleeping on their fat bellies in the alleyway. But then they too woke up and sniffed the air, as if bad luck had an odor to it.

Ground
Squirrels

The first thing the boys did to get ground squirrels in the pasture was to find all the holes. This way one boy could pour the cream cans of water down one hole while the others waited at the dry holes with sticks.

Not everybody could get ground squirrels this way. You had to know what you were doing. If you poured the water down too slow, the ground would soak it up before it got to the ground squirrel. If you made too much noise near the opening of the hole where you were going to pour the water, the ground squirrel might dam it up a few feet down the tunnel. You had to be quiet and you had to be fast. And you had to have a lot of water. If the water wasn't coming fast enough and if there was not enough of it, the ground squirrel would try to drink it as it came. But if it heard and felt a tidal wave coming, it ran for light with no questions asked.

There was one big old ground squirrel the boys had been trying to get all summer. One time it must have heard them coming and dammed up the hole. When the boys tried pouring water in another hole, it beat them by damming that one up too. It must have followed their footsteps from hole to hole, damming each one up just before the boys could pour water down it. Another time the boys were quiet enough, but the squirrel dug a low passage that emptied into the creek letting all the water run away while it remained safely in the higher tunnels. Another time right after the water was poured in one hole, it poked its head out of another. But this was just to distract the boys, who all came running over to that hole with their sticks while the squirrel made a quick escape out of another hole behind their backs. Getting that ground squirrel had become the project of the summer.

This time we're going to use five cans of water instead of three, said the oldest boy. We're going to make sure there are no low holes where the water will run out, we're going to be perfectly quiet. And we're not going to let it trick us by sticking its head out of one hole and coming out of another.

The boys watched for two afternoons before they saw the ground squirrel out in the open. It had grown even bigger than the last time they had seen it. One of the grown-ups saw it too and said it was the biggest one he had ever seen. That critter must eat fifty dollars worth of corn a year. I'll give each of you a dollar if you get that one, he said.

Now the boys knew they had to get the ground squirrel for sure. There was more than pride at stake. There was money. They waited and waited, watching it move from one part of the pasture to another until finally just before supper it went down a hole. Not only did the boys walk quietly, but they took only a few steps at a time, and then stopped a few seconds. The way a cow does when it is grazing. If the squirrel was going to hear them, they wanted it to think the sound was just that of a harmless cow. The littlest boy bent down when they were pausing and pulled off a few handfuls of grass to make their presence sound even more like a grazing cow.

When everyone was in place, one of the boys poured all five cans of water down the hole as fast as he could. The boys at the other holes were ready with their sticks and could even hear air coming out, the water was filling up the tunnels that fast!

Everything was going according to plan! Everyone was frozen in his place and ready. It would only be a matter of a few seconds now, they were sure of it. Then one of the boys heard a swishing sound in the grass. He turned his head. It was only a curious cow swishing her tail. Then he heard another swishing sound on the other side and turned, expecting another cow. But there was no cow. Then there was another swishing sound a little farther away, and there was no other cow. But the grass was moving. And the boys were already starting to blush.

❀

What Are
They Missing?

There was a kind of boar that went on breeding even after it was castrated. It had a hidden testicle that could not be found or seen, and there was no way of telling which boar was keeping this potent secret.

But it was no secret when that animal set itself to work on young gilts that were meant for market instead of breeding.

Look! That one has a hidden testicle! one of the men would shout, and everyone would jump helter-skelter into the pig pen with sticks and feed scoops, smacking and pushing the busy boar off the female before any damage was done.

The men separated this kind of boar from the other pigs, but the boys noticed how the men, instead of punishing that animal, gave it more and better feed than the others. Once the boys watched a man stand next to the animal's special pen for nearly an hour, talking quietly to it and stooping over now and then to stroke its ears.

For the boys, the mystery was not so much in the strange boar as in the men. After all, where their own testicles were located was perfectly ordinary. What do the men think they are missing? the boys wondered.

Who Wore Twine around His Pants Legs

Young male sheep were luckier than young boars. Men castrated the young pigs but only slipped small rubber bands around the scrotums of male lambs to keep them from breeding.

The lambs were only a few days old when this happened to them and in a week or two the testicles fell off like dry umbilical cords. The lambs didn't even notice it.

When the boys fought with each other, sometimes one of them said to another, I'm going to put a rubber band around your nuts while you're sleeping.

One day one of the boys woke up with an awful itch. He figured someone had put a rubber band over his scrotum while he was sleeping.

He looked but could not see the rubber band. He used a

flashlight, a tweezers, but the rubber band had already disappeared under the skin.

What if they fall off and somebody finds them? he thought. Everyone will hear about it!

He took care of this worry by tying twine around his pants legs. This way when his testicles fell off he'd be the only one who could find them and nobody else would have to know.

There was only one problem. The twine kept coming loose, and he was always bending down to tie it again. It was a real nuisance.

Would it have been better, he wondered after many weeks of constant stooping, to have lost my balls like a lamb before I even knew I had any than to waste half my life like this trying to save them?

Sleight of Hand

Labor Day was one of those times when many boys got together at the same place. It was among their favorite holidays because at that time of the year the corn was tall and green and made a good place to sneak off to while the grown-ups settled down on lawn chairs and blankets with their stomachs full of potato salad and ham sandwiches.

Some boy would have a corncob pipe and there was always some corn silk brown and dry enough to smoke. One game was getting a younger boy to inhale corn-silk smoke so that he would cough and make a fool of himself. Then there would be a game of tag and some wrestling and pretty soon everyone was tired and sitting down and someone would say, Let's jack off.

Usually a boy old enough to have pubic hair said this and got things started. The younger boys found ways of holding their hands so that no one could see that they did not have any hair yet. One clever boy even learned a trick of pulling some hair from his head without anyone seeing him. He wadded it into his palm and then, while pretending to go after his penis, he spread it down where the pubic hair would grow some day. He was so good at this that he could keep the hair in place and make a good show for himself.

Most of the boys were pretty impressed by the young boy with false pubic hair. Until one Labor Day he was found out. He probably would never have been caught if it had not been for the fact that he was also very good at card tricks. He could hide cards up his sleeve or in his palm and who knows where else. The other boys admired his fast hands so much when he was doing card tricks that they started watching them closer in the cornfield too. And, sure enough, one Labor Day an older boy who had been most impressed with his card tricks said, Look, he's got hair growing in his palm.

The younger boy, who was almost as quick with his tongue as he was with his hands, said, Oh, that's just because I jack off so much.

But then a breeze caught the little wadded-up ball of hair and sent it flying like a tuft of corn silk. Those gusty winds that come whipping through cornfields on Labor Day have shown up more than one lie. Still, the boy's clever remark took hold in that neighborhood and pretty soon even the grown-ups were saying to boys that if they played with themselves hair would grow from their palms. Maybe people are even saying this in your neighborhood and you have wondered where the story got started.

❀

In Which
the Librarian
Writes a Letter
to the Editor

There weren't many outdoor privies left. Ones that didn't rot from age were tipped over on Halloween nights by teen-age boys. And the owners of the few that did remain did everything they could to outsmart the boys who were trying to figure out ways to tip them over.

One very mean farmer looked out for his privy with a big machete that he flashed around town on Halloween day.

I'm going to wait inside my privy with this thing, he said, and chop up anyone who comes near it.

Some boys fixed him by taking a long rope and running with five boys on either end until the rope came across the rear of the privy. Keeping their distance this way, they tipped the privy onto its front door before the man with the machete even heard them coming. The only way he could get out was through the seat holes, which meant falling into the pit.

The toilet-tippers didn't always get the last laugh. One clever farmer moved his privy ahead six feet so that when boys came up behind to tip it on Halloween night, they fell into the hole.

There were so many tricks that privy owners and boys played on each other that a book could be written about it.

But the only person who wrote anything about it in those parts was the town librarian. She was a spinster who always looked angry, but she usually didn't say what she was thinking. She wrote a letter to the editor which was printed in the newspaper. She said it was terrible the fuss people made over outhouses on Halloween. She was bothered, she wrote, by the scatological obsession of our youth. That's what she wrote to the paper: *scatological obsession of our youth*!

Most people didn't understand her letter, but the boys figured out that she didn't like what they did to outhouses on Halloween nights.

Too bad for the librarian, she had an outhouse too. And hers was not old and rotting. Hers was quite new and the only toilet she had. She lived a simple life of order and neatness. Her outhouse was so neat and clean that many people didn't even know it was her toilet.

But the boys did. And what she wrote in the newspaper gave them an idea. They started with forty squares of active yeast. They shoved these down into the librarian's toilet with broom handles. And like the world's greatest loaf of bread, the toilet contents did begin to rise. And rise. First it came up through the toilet seat holes, and then lifted the neat little shanty into the air. The yeast kept working until some people said the raised privy looked like a steeple on top of that big mound.

The newspaper printed a picture and a caption which read: *Local librarian discovers scatology on the rise, as shown in this backyard photograph.*

Blondy's Calf

The men were standing near the silo shuffling their feet and not looking at each other. The boys could tell something was wrong. They walked over to the men and one of the boys asked, What's the matter?

Blondy slipped her calf, said one of the men.

The fetus was lying near the fence where the men had thrown it. The boys went over to look more closely. It didn't look like a calf. The head was round like a Raggedy-Ann doll's. The face was flat instead of long and had two nostril holes in the middle. The ears were short and round. It had regular hoofs but there wasn't any hair on the body. The fetus looked more like a human being than a calf.

Now the boys started shuffling their feet and didn't look at each other. They didn't point fingers at anybody, but the oldest boy could feel what the others were thinking. Blondy saw the boys and walked over to the fence where they were looking at her fetus. She put her head between the barbed wires and tried to lick her offspring, but then lifted her wet nose to the boys as she always did when she wanted to be petted or fed. The boys looked at the men and stepped back from her. Had the men noticed how much the calf did not look like a calf? But then they figured it would be all right to feed and pet Blondy in front of the men. They probably knew that Blondy was the tamest cow and wouldn't think anything of it.

The
Good Luck
Necklace

When the old bitch had another litter of pups, the men guessed there were as many fathers as there were offspring because none of the pups looked alike.

She must have run with a pack of wild dogs when she was in heat. You'd never guess these critters were brothers and sisters.

The boys listened to the men talk about the bad breeding in that litter and were afraid the men were going to kill the pups. And they had to admit that the litter looked pretty bad. Some were spotted and some were solid; one had big paws and the others small; some had brown eyes and the others blue; some had short noses and some had long. But the biggest difference was in the tails. The tails were all different colors and shapes. When the pups were nursing, the boys saw the wagging tails did not match at all.

Let's cut the tails off. That will make them look alike, said the oldest boy.

The others agreed it was a good idea, so they took the pups one at a time to the chopping block. The oldest boy had the ax, but he was so afraid of cutting into the pups' hindquarters that he swung wide and chopped off only the tips of their tails. When he was finished, the blunt tail ends made the pups look even worse.

When the men saw how foolish the pups looked, they pitied the boys for trying so hard to save them and promised not to kill any.

This did not make the pups look any better, but it did make the boys proud of what they had done. So proud that they found all the tail tips and strung them on a cord as a good luck necklace.

The Rat
Cage Trap

There was a wire cage trap for catching rats. It was a kinder way of catching rats than the regular trap which clamped down on one of their legs and tortured them until they were put out of their misery.

But once the boys took a cage trap with a rat in it and set it on a fire they built from corncobs. When the rat saw the fire, it got nervous and ran around the cage squeaking like a toy rubber mouse. The rat tried to climb the side of the cage when the boys put the cage on the fire, and even hung upside down on the top for a moment. But the flames still got to it and made its hair curl like tiny springs. It lost all its sense and ran right into the hottest part of the fire. It stood still, clinging to the cage while the fire did its work. Then it stiffened quickly as if it had gotten a shock, and the boys shoved the cage off the fire before the smell was too strong for them.

Only after the thing was done did the boys get nervous. They tipped the rat out on the ground and one of them took it on a spade and hurried to bury it in the grove. Others ran for water to put out the fire. Then they took the cage down to the stock tank and washed off all the charcoal and rat skin, looking around all the while to see if anyone was watching. When everything was back in place and looked normal, they went into the house.

When the grown-ups saw them, the boys tried to act as if nothing had happened, but the grown-ups could tell they had been up to something.

What have you been doing?

Nothing, said one of the boys.

Then the grown-ups started guessing. Have you been picking apples again before they are ripe? You'd better not have run the calves through the fence again.

Pretty soon the boys admitted that they had done something that one of the grown-ups suggested they might have done. This way they could look guilty while the grown-ups scolded and warned and shook their fingers. It was not much fun but it did give them some time to get that rat off their minds.

Firecrackers

It was almost the Fourth of July and the boys had big fire-crackers they were blowing off. Let's stick one up a chick-en's ass! said one of the boys.

They did this terrible thing and blew the bottom out of a chicken. It hobbled away bleeding. It hid under the corn-crib, and died there.

The same night they decided to tie a firecracker to the leg of a sparrow, light the fuse, and let the sparrow fly away. As it flew sparkling into the night, they pointed sticks at it and BANG! they yelled when the sparrow blew up in the night sky. As if the sticks were guns and the sparrow was an air-plane they had shot.

A few days later at the Fourth of July celebration the boys laughed when the crowd sang *The Star-Spangled Banner* at the line, bombs bursting in air. This was during a time of war and the boys could not feel bad about the chicken and sparrow, especially now when everyone's spirits were up while they were singing together.

Nature's Way

When it was time to butcher roosters, the men told the younger boys to catch the roosters and the oldest boy to chop the heads off. The oldest boy was happy to have the most important job and ran to get the ax. But when he came back he could not find the chopping block.

Everyone started looking, but then someone remembered. We burned the chopping block in the old cook stove last winter when the oil furnace went off.

I can't chop the roosters' heads off without a chopping block, said the oldest boy to the men. You'd better make me another one.

Let's see now, said one of the men. That old cherry stump got rotted out, didn't it? And those willows aren't big enough. And we sold that oak log two years ago, didn't we? And we cleared out that stand of ash to make room for more corn. Everyone looked around. There were not any logs left on the farm. And there were not any trees left that were big enough to make a chopping block.

You'll just have to figure out a new way of doing it, said one of the men, and they left to do the fieldwork.

The oldest boy ran to the house and returned with a butcher knife and a new plan. One of you hold the wings and feet, he said. I'll grab the head and cut it off with the butcher knife. The youngest boy held the rooster, but just when the oldest had cut through the neck, the wings and legs beat so hard that the decapitated rooster got loose and jumped wildly in the air, spraying blood over everyone and getting bloody mud all over itself when it hit the ground.

This is not going to work, said the oldest boy. The cutting part is easy, but a rooster is real hard to hang on to when its head is cut off.

So the oldest boy figured out a way to give each boy the right job to match his strength. He held the rooster, most of the other boys did the catching, and the youngest boy cut off the heads.

Later the men came around to see how the boys were doing. The youngest boy's arms were covered with blood and he had gotten very quick and sure of himself with the knife. There were baskets filled with dead roosters ready to be carried away for the women to skin.

The men saw that the boys had found a plan that was working out just fine. Isn't it something, the way nature takes care of itself if you just leave it alone, marveled one of the men.

Part III

If the
Weather
Stayed Nice

Isn't it wonderful the way the ducks fly south for the winter! exclaimed an old woman who always saw the best side of nature.

What's so wonderful about it? said Uncle Jack. If the weather stayed nice, they wouldn't have to go through all that trouble flying south.

The old woman ruffled her shawl. If the weather stayed nice, she said in a mocking voice. If the weather stayed nice! Don't you know that flying south makes the ducks strong and healthy?

Flying south keeps them from getting their tails frozen in the ice is what it does, said Uncle Jack. If the weather stayed nice, the ducks could spend their time swimming in the quiet ponds. Or preening themselves. Or learning how to sing. Instead of their miserable quacking, maybe they'd sit and listen to themselves and learn how to carry a tune.

Carry a tune! shouted the old woman, fluttering a little. Quacking is their own beautiful music! She waddled toward Uncle Jack, and she might have attacked him if it had not been for a cold November breeze which caught the back of her neck. It stunned her old body and brought out a horrendous sneeze. She looked behind her to see the huge black cloud that was rolling in from the north. She tried flapping her flabby arms, but her old body stood there quivering.

Uncle Jack
and the Ducks

One summer day Uncle Jack came to visit the boys. They remembered how stupid he acted from last year's visit when he did not know how to fasten his shoelaces and had his hat on backwards.

Maybe he has grown some brains since last year, one of the boys suggested. After Uncle Jack had some coffee with the grown-ups, the boys decided to test him.

Uncle Jack, would you like to see the pigs?

Oh, yes, he said. I would like that very much, and he wiped one of his big ears with his handkerchief.

Instead of leading Uncle Jack to the pigpens, the boys led him to the pond where the ducks were. The ducks started to quack as the boys came nearer with Uncle Jack.

They certainly sound like pigs, said Uncle Jack.

Oh, you wait and see, said one boy and led Uncle Jack closer.

My goodness, they're walking on two little yellow legs with webbed feet, just the way pigs do, said Uncle Jack.

One duck opened its bill for some food.

Oh, look at that mouth, said Uncle Jack, just the right size for a nice healthy pig.

All our pigs are like that, explained the boys.

Why, I declare, said Uncle Jack who then sat on a fence post and sang the boys this song:

> The pig is swimming like a duck
> and if it has a preacher's luck
> 'twill soon grow wings upon its back
> and learn to quack,
> yes, quack quack quack.

> A pig that waddles like a duck?
> Do old drakes wallow in the muck?
> If my name is Uncle Jack
> a pig can quack
> yes, quack quack quack.

> If ducks are pigs, then up is down,
> the swill is blue and the sky is brown,
> a needle is bigger than your aunt's haystack,
> if pigs can quack
> yes, quack quack quack.

> If you get there before I do
> with your feet in a hat and your head in a shoe,
> at a place where the snow is midnight black

and pigs go quack,
yes, quack quack quack,

Be sure you forget to sing this song
with a long one short and a short one long—
smile a smile behind your back
and the pigs will quack,
yes, quack quack quack.

Sing another song! Sing another song! shouted the boys.

Not right now, said Uncle Jack.

And with that he barked twice at the pigs before fluttering off down the road, bits of down wafting up from his shaggy coat.

See you next year, Uncle Jack! shouted the boys who had their own brains to look after.

Uncle Jack's
Riddle

Uncle Jack had a way of appearing when he was least expected. Since he was not known for his good sense, it did
not surprise anyone that he was unpredictable. No one
knew what day Uncle Jack might show up—but then, he
probably did not either.

Hello there! came a voice through the boys' bedroom
window early one very rainy summer morning. The boys
were very jittery since thunder and lightning had been coming and going all evening. Hearing that voice between claps
of thunder was enough to startle them to their wits' end.

Hello there! came the voice again. It's a good day for mud
pies!

The boys ran to the window. It was Uncle Jack! There he
stood in the drive, wearing a black raincoat with a big hood

on it. He looked more like a bear standing upright than like a human being.

Do you know what can go out in the rain without a cap on and not get its head wet? he shouted up to them.

It was another one of Uncle Jack's silly riddles. The oldest boy said, Uncle Jack, did you really come all the way over here through the thunderstorm just to ask that stupid riddle?

A duck, interrupted the youngest boy. That was an easy riddle, Uncle Jack.

Wrong, little one. Not everything can be a duck. You guessed too quickly this time, said Uncle Jack. Now you'll have to listen to all the clues. And, still standing in the rain, Uncle Jack sang the whole riddle to the boys.

> I have no legs,
> I have no arms,
> I wear no bracelets
> for my charms.

> I have no eyes,
> I have no nose,
> and when I rise,
> I wear no clothes.

> No whiskers have I,
> though I do have hair,
> when I appear,
> young women stare.

> I start out small,
> but then I swell,

not like the wind
or a steeple bell.

When the rains come down,
my head stays dry,
without a rain cap—
now what am I?

The boys could not think of any answers to Uncle Jack's riddle. What is it, Uncle Jack? We give up.

Why, it's a thunderhead, said Uncle Jack. I've been watching them all night. There's nothing but stars above them and it only rains beneath them, so the thunderhead must always be dry.

Uncle Jack chuckled and said, Whoever tells that riddle, his mouth will always be warm. With that he ran laughing down the drive.

The boys looked out the window at the large thunderheads. Say, said one of the boys, they don't have hair. Uncle Jack's riddle said,

No whiskers have I
but I do have hair.

Just then the sky lit up again with long wavy strands of lightning that reached to the ground.

Then there was thunder, which sounded very much like Uncle Jack's crazy laughter.

Uncle Jack
and the Compass

The boys went into town one Saturday night and met Uncle Jack at the Laundromat. It was the one place in town where the gum machine sometimes gave little prizes, and when they met Uncle Jack there he always gave each of them a coin to try their luck. But, as usual, it was only Uncle Jack who got a prize with his gum, this time a small compass with the figure of a duck on it. The head of the duck was the needle, pointing north. The boys got only gum and were jealous of Uncle Jack for his good luck.

You always get everything, said one of the boys. You're everybody's pet. You're even the gum machine's pet.

But Uncle Jack was not listening. He laid his little compass on his palm and followed the N arrow across the Laundromat. It pointed him toward the only washing machine that was in use. It had a round porthole of a window, and clothing churned and bounced against the glass. An old fat woman stood next to the washing machine with her clothes basket. She was watching her clothes through the little porthole.

The old woman wore dirty tennis shoes and brown stockings rolled down around her ankles to look like dog collars. There were crusted scabs on her legs where she might have scratched mosquito or flea bites. Her dress was faded pink and looked as if it had been tan or white once and then washed with red. Her breasts were large and hung down, but she had her arms crossed in front of her and held them up. They bulged over her forearms and almost covered them. Her wrinkled face was spotted with moles and dark patches. She had her gray hair tied up on her head, but strands of it had come loose and hung like little broken branches over her ears.

Uncle Jack stood next to her with his compass and looked into the washing machine too. Inside were nothing but panties, brassieres, and underskirts. And they were bright flashy colors with flower designs. Red roses and yellow pansies bounced against the window of the machine.

And who are you, my pet? asked the old woman.

I'm the lucky one, said Uncle Jack. I got a compass with my gum.

And what are you looking for, my lucky one? said the old woman, letting down her arms and breasts.

I'm looking for North, he said.

And has your lucky compass found it in my washing machine? she asked.

Well, if flowers fly north in the spring, he said. It seems to be attracted this way.

The old woman chuckled and drooled a little. Yes, yes, she said. Flowers fly north in the spring. As she laughed, more and more pieces of flowered underwear appeared, some falling from under her arms, some from under her dress. The boys moved toward the door, chewing on what little they had, but Uncle Jack stood watching the needle of his compass persist while the old woman went on shedding colorful underwear like petals.

Uncle Jack
and the Beautiful
Schoolteacher

Uncle Jack went to meet the beautiful schoolteacher who lived in a mobile home on the school yard. He had seen her downtown shopping and noticed how gracefully her hands moved across the fabric in the dry goods store and how delicate their movement as she lifted an apple to the light in the supermarket. He felt there was a message to him in the way she touched things, but he was not sure what it was.

As Uncle Jack approached her small metal trailer house, he saw her outside hanging her wash on a rope which had been strung to a nearby tree. Even now, her hands seemed to dance like those of a deaf person talking to a lover. When she saw him, she stopped her work and smiled. Yes, she recognized him too.

You have very special hands, said Uncle Jack.

I have noticed yours too, she said. They stood in the cool

sunlight of that October day staring at each other's hands. After a few moments of this admiration, she held up her right hand in such a way that the shadow of a rose appeared on the shining white side of the trailer house.

Ah, yes, what a wonderful projection screen, said Uncle Jack. The petals of the shadow-rose quivered as if responding to the same breeze which was bringing color to their cheeks where they stood side by side. Then across the white screen came the shadow of Uncle Jack's right hand in the form of a butterfly which lit pulsing on the rose. Then like a second movie being projected on the same screen, her left hand formed in such a way that its shadow became a rabbit. As quickly, Uncle Jack's left hand made the shadow of a carrot which dangled over the rabbit's nose and which the rabbit, in what seemed to be a natural and instinctive move, sat up to nibble. But even as the rabbit of her left hand was eating, the petals of her rose hand faded from under the fluttering wings of his butterfly and became a mare galloping across a plain, but his butterfly shadow turned into a saddle which her mare could not throw off. The left-handed rabbit shadow now became a sunfish swimming through shimmering water. But his devoured carrot-hand became a net which caught the fish. While on the right, her mare pretended to stumble on the plain only to rise a palm tree on a desert. Sensing that an oasis was near, his discarded saddle became a camel which paused to rub its humped back on the trunk of her palm tree. Meanwhile, the left-handed shadow of a fish slipped through the loose net of his fingers and emerged as a sailboat driven by a wind which their reddening faces showed had grown stronger. But Uncle Jack's net became the ocean itself carrying the blithe boat on its undulant swells. Still the branches of her right hand wavered in the desert sun until without warning it was the shadow of a sand dune which could have been a rippling mirage of water. But Uncle Jack's camel, wise to the desert, became the wind which caressed the dune as a hand might caress a breast. The sailboat shadow of her left hand had taken wings and was a duck ascending toward an open window of her trailer house. From the dark shadow of that window came the shadow of Uncle Jack's hand, a cloud which engulfed the bird. The sand dune, still changing shape with the wind of his right hand, became itself, her hand shadowed, connected to the shadow of her arm, and as she turned, the wind turned lifting her hair unfurling into a shadow of fire on her head, and the duck of her left hand fell through the cloud of his shadow as rain which, falling, crystallized into fingers, and then her other hand, and she was totally the shadow of herself, and he himself, his shadow, and his hands moved no less gently from his larger body, though both of them were fading in the shadow of a huge cloud which the wind had carried overhead until, their shadows gone, they had to turn to each other and what was left of them, the flesh and bone, an echo of that other life which had sunk into the larger shadow which contained them.

Part IV

The
Good Hider

This woman liked to hide from her husband. It is not that she did not like him, and she did not have to be in an angry or sad mood when she hid. She just needed to be in a hiding mood. It could happen any time. Maybe the husband would come home from the fields and she would not be in the house. Or he might turn over in his sleep to be awakened by the cold place on the sheet where she should have been. Then he would go down to his easy chair to see if she had hung her apron on it. This was her way of telling him that everything was all right but that she had gone off to hide.

Right away the husband would start his hunt. She would leave him a few clues. Maybe a kerchief on a fence she had climbed. Or a barn door left open just a bit. Like a little grin. But after that she was a good hider. She was good at making herself look like the place she was hiding. On sunny days when her long hair was blond in the sunlight, she might hide near the straw stack where her hair would look the same color as the straw. On a rainy day she might hide in a willow tree where her long wet hair would hang down to look like wet willow branches. Or she would stand in the shape of a small apple tree in the orchard with an apple in each of her outstretched hands. Other times she would hide among animals, making herself look and sound like them. Once she hid in a pen of sleeping sows, lying down among them with her hands and feet in front of her like the legs of a sow. And she made the snoring noises of the sows so well that the animals did not notice that she was there among them.

But the husband was as good a seeker as the wife was a hider. He knew how to look and listen for what was not there: like the branch that should have been moving in the wind, or swallows that should have been singing, or crickets that should have been chirping. He would walk on the paths that seemed least walked-on and would stop and listen at those places which seemed least listened-to. When he thought he was getting warm, he stood still and held his breath. If she was holding her breath, he would hold his longer. If she was making sounds of the animals nearby, he would hear the little giggle that was not the sound of an animal.

And when she was found out, she would leap up or down from her hiding place. Like a flushed partridge or pouncing cat. She came at him wild and laughing. Even when he was expecting it, she scared him, and he would turn away running as fast as he could. She always caught him in a few steps. As he knew she would. Just as she knew he would find her.

The
Old Waitress

A very old waitress with a long gray braid worked in the café. Men who came there over the years joked about the gray braid because its color never changed and it never got any longer or shorter. They knew it was a fake. Sometimes they could even see where the bobby pins held it to the back of her head. But the braid was not the only thing about this waitress that did not change. When customers walked in, she always greeted them with the same word. She always said, Order?

There were many ways the men could answer that question. Like

Order be a law against this weather.

or Order in the court!

or Order day I drunk too much.

The old waitress did not smile or answer when the men

joked about order. She would not even look at them until they ordered food. Some men thought she secretly liked their jokes about order, but most of them figured she was as ornery as she looked with her fake braid cutting the air behind her like a cattle whip.

Then the old waitress did something no one expected. She died. Now the men joked about her fake braid. Hey, did you hear?—the old waitress hung up her braid.

But when those men went back to the café, it was closed. And the very ones who joked about the braid stood in front of the café, looked quietly at the sign.

It was in her own handwriting, and it said, *Out of Order*.

The Meddler

Maybe if you had lace curtains your living room wouldn't be so dark, said the meddler to a woman who did not yet know about her. I know where there were some on sale last week. Should I telephone and see if they have any left? If you give me the money, I could go down and get them for you.

Oh, I couldn't put you through all that trouble, said the unsuspecting victim.

No trouble at all, said the meddler. I could pick up some rug shampoo for this carpet too, if you would like.

Oh, that would be very nice, actually, said the victim who had just noticed that the meddler had left her purse open on her couch. What do you think of that wall? asked the victim. Do you think it is too pink? She pointed to distract the meddler while reaching into her purse for the loose ten and five.

Indeed it is too pink, said the meddler. You could much better go toward a cream, which would brighten this room up more too. Should I see if they have any paint specials while I am down getting your lace curtains?

That would be nice, said the victim, palming the bills. If there is anything that needs doing at your house, I would be happy to give you a hand in return, said the victim. I may not be a good planner like you, but I do have good hands.

How very generous of you, said the meddler. I think we could become friends.

So do I, said the victim, reaching to shake the hand of the meddler which was adorned with a diamond ring. Let's have a cup of tea to celebrate.

Wonderful idea, said the meddler.

Together they walked into the kitchen, the meddler intrigued by the possibilities of remodelling the hallway, the victim intrigued by the gold chain around the meddler's neck, which she knew she could remove if only she could get the meddler to stoop over.

Who Talked
in His Sleep

Everyone who knew him thought he was a kind and gentle person. But his wife knew another person came out when he talked in his sleep.

Do you know what you said last night? she asked him one morning when he awoke.

I dreamt that we were hiding in a cave along the coast, he said.

That is not what you talked about, she said.

The husband looked at her with his kind and gentle eyes. Could this really be the man she heard saying, Cut her head off. There. Now slit open her stomach. She did not dare to tell him what he had said in his sleep. She imagined how disturbed he might become if he knew the horror of his words. Never, she thought, will I do anything to undo his kind and gentle manner.

You told me you loved me, said the wife. And the husband, believing her, tenderly embraced her and offered to bring her breakfast in bed.

The next night the wife awakened to hear him say, Give me the knife. You are bungling the job. I do not like unnecessary blood. She touched his arm, hoping to awaken him, but his muscles tightened as if under the strain of a difficult task.

If we cannot cut her up neatly, we could just as well not cut her up at all, he added with great authority between his deep breathing and occasional snores.

In the morning the wife asked him if he was happy with her or if there was anything about her that he would like to change.

I only wish you were as beautiful in my dreams as you are in real life, he said, touching her cheek in his kind and gentle way.

The
Stingy Man

Down the road lived a stingy man. Instead of getting his dog spayed after she had more puppies than he wanted, he drowned the new litter. Water is cheaper than the veterinarian, he said. He took the dead puppies and buried them in his garden. He said they made his vegetables grow better. Dead puppies are cheaper than fertilizer, he said.

But the dog was a good mother and dug up her puppies. She laid them neatly in front of her doghouse where she could give them a bath. All six of them. She was licking them clean when the stingy man found her. Her big paw on the stomach of the one she was cleaning, the same way she would do it if the puppy were alive and trying to wriggle away. The stingy man dragged the dead puppies away from her and buried them in a different place in the garden. She dug them up again, but again the stingy man buried them, this time in still another spot in the garden. They did this over and over, each time the mother digging up her puppies and the stingy man burying them in the garden. After a while the whole garden had been weeded in this way. Dead puppies are cheaper than a new cultivator, said the stingy man.

The Girl
Who Was Always
Tardy

What do you think will happen when you grow up and always come to work late?

What if all the kids came to school late—we wouldn't be able to have school, would we?

How do you think it makes other people feel when they invite you over and you don't care enough about them to show up on time?

If God wanted you to come late to everything, He would make the sun stand still for an hour so you could catch up with everybody else, wouldn't He?

If I love you enough to make these nice hot meals, why can't you at least show enough respect to show up for dinner on time?

What do you think would happen if firemen weren't on time?

Now then, young lady, we want some answers.

If you really want them you'll wait for them, said the girl.

The
Neat Woman

There was a woman who was very neat. Whatever she cleaned once, she cleaned twice, whether it was her dishes or her fingernails. When she had finished washing the windows twice, she would wash the car twice. When she finished with the car she swept the floor twice, perhaps stopping only for a few seconds to reload the clean clothes into the washing machine.

This woman was doing fine in her neat way until she started to grow older. It was not that she started to lose her strength. It was just that her world kept growing bigger. First there was one child to keep doubly clean, but then there were two which meant four scrubbings for every after-breakfast cleanup. And then there were three children which meant six scrubbings. As the family grew, the house grew too with double the space to clean twice. Then there were two cars with two instead of one windshield to wash twice. The hedge around the yard grew larger over the years and the apple trees grew and the number of dishes grew. There continued to become more and more places where the neat woman had to be twice at the same time.

You'll just have to stop being so neat! said her husband who had grown thin over the years from watching her.

I'm not neat, I'm not neat, said the neat woman, but she really did not have time to argue with him because the world was filling up with dirt behind her.

Then a volcano went off somewhere and volcanic dust settled over everything the neat woman kept clean.

This should change your mind, said the husband from behind his dust mask.

But the neat woman thought of this as the challenge of her life. She dusted and dusted and swept and swept and scrubbed and scrubbed, but the sky kept falling.

It is not natural for you to do this, the husband said, trying to subdue his neat wife.

The volcano is not natural, the volcano is not natural, said the neat woman. And she went on against the odds of the gray flaking sky until one day, even while her hands were covered with soap suds, she turned into dust like the sky, and everything seemed to have its way, though nothing seemed to have won.

The Man
with
Smart Hands

This man could not figure anything out unless he put his hands on it. You could tell him a hundred times and draw him a hundred pictures, but if he could not touch it he could not understand it. He was a good carpenter so long as you did not give him a blueprint, and he was a good mechanic so long as you did not show him a repair manual. But anything that had to go through his head before it went through his hands did not get anywhere with him.

Most people figured the man was just stupid and at best they pitied him. Then one year a beautiful and intelligent woman came to that neighborhood to teach school. A few months later she married him. What is going on? the people wondered. Why would anyone so smart and pretty marry a fool?

The schoolteacher heard what people were saying, and

one day at the meat market she spoke up. Some people have smart heads, she said, and some people have smart hands.

She looked as if she might give a long speech, and no doubt she could have because she was a very clever woman. But instead she just stood there in front of the people who turned from the meat counter to listen. She started to blush, first her face, then her arms and neck. To those who looked closely she seemed to break into bloom like a red tulip. The butcher smiled and nodded. Many others were also pleased with what they saw, and left feeling better about both the woman and her husband. But a few were only confused and guessed that the man's stupidity had gone to the woman's head too.

Gas

Hold your nose! Here he comes!

In church, when he was preaching, there was a safe distance between him and the congregation. The air conditioning may also have helped. Occasionally, the microphone which he wore on his tie picked up an inadvertent sound or two, but the congregation had gotten used to this, and there was no way the radio audience could have known what it was.

But during the week when he was doing his pastorly duties, he often passed gas at especially bad times. Such as while visiting the sick. Or at a wedding when the groom and his bride in pristine white gown were kneeling before him. Or at social occasions, especially dinner parties which were held indoors.

One old man in the congregation thought the flatulent

pastor was unfit for the ministry. What he does in people's presence is a sin. By their fruits shall ye know them, he said.

Elders in the church brought the man's accusations to the minister. May the fire of my soul be equal to the fire of my bowels, he said. Bring this man to me. And for a moment the air in that small consistory room was clear and silent.

What do you know of spiritual matters? the minister asked the old man sternly.

I know that it is not what proceedeth into a man but what proceedeth from him which defileth him, he said, holding his Bible in his hands.

The stench of your heart is filling this room, said the minister. Do not ye yet understand, that whatsoever entereth in at the mouth goeth into the belly, and is cast into the draft? But those things which proceed out of the mouth come from the heart; and *they* defile the man. The minister opened the Bible to Matthew 15:16–17, which the old man had misquoted.

And with that he passed gas heartily. There, he said emphatically. At that moment the old man's heart was opened. He knew he was in the presence of a holy man whose very life was a parable.

The
Critical Woman

There was a woman who was very critical. She could spot what someone had done wrong before the person who had done it even realized it. Her friends and relatives were always a little bit afraid when she came around because they knew she would see something wrong with what they were doing. It would have been easy for other people to deal with the critical woman if her criticism were silly. They might be able to say, Oh well, she finds something wrong with almost everything and everybody—no sense paying any attention to her. But such was not the case. The problem for everyone was that the critical woman had a way of being right. And they knew it.

It was an odd year which meant that the critical woman's family would be having a big family reunion. Her relatives got more and more nervous as the day of the reunion got closer. They started phoning each other and discussing what to wear and what kind of food to bring. And after they had decided on which food and which clothes, they called each other again to discuss how to cook the food and how to wear the clothes. What shade of makeup will look best with my turquoise pantsuit? one woman asked. If I wear my white tennis shoes, can I still wear colored socks? one man asked. And what about our children? How can we be sure they will behave in appropriate ways? Is there time to retrain them? And who is qualified to do the retraining?

The critical woman did not know she caused such a stir just by being who she was. As the day of the family reunion approached, she spent many hours alone in her sewing room. She did not worry about what people would think of *her*. She did not worry about how they would react to the food *she* brought or to the clothing *she* wore. But she did worry about being helpful. She was not exactly a religious woman, but she did like to offer her talents to other people. And, so far as she was able to tell, her greatest talent was in seeing what others were doing wrong. Sometimes, sitting alone and thinking, she could feel her love for others grow in her chest like the silver lining around an expanding rain cloud. How can I serve them best? she would whisper to herself.

A few weeks before the big reunion, the critical woman decided to make a list of topics on which she felt she could best offer advice to her relatives:

> Dress and Personal Appearance
> Food and Its Proper Preparation
> Child Nurturing and Discipline
> Grammar and Elocution
> Manners and Personal Habits

Good Health and How to Achieve It
How to Sit, Stand, or Walk Properly
How to Manage your Finances
How to Get Along with People
Good Housekeeping: Cleanliness and Order.

She attached a note to this list which read, PLEASE LET ME KNOW ON WHICH OF THESE TOPICS YOU WOULD MOST LIKE ADVICE. Then she sent each of her relatives a copy.

There were perhaps forty more topics the critical woman could think of, but the family reunion was only for one day, and she did not want to offer so much advice that they would not be able to remember all of it and use it in their lives.

When her relatives received the note, they were all more frightened than ever. There were items on the list that they had not even thought of! Now they had even more to worry about. They phoned and phoned, asking each other for advice. Finally, they decided to choose a spokesperson to send the critical woman a note asking her not to criticize any of them at the family reunion for anything. Please! We're all scared of you, the return note said.

When the critical woman got the note, she could not believe her eyes. Not that she did not try to sympathize with her relatives' point of view—it was just that the note was so poorly written, the handwriting atrocious, the choice of stationery ridiculous, and her street address on the envelope misspelled. The critical woman spent an extra day making notes in preparation for the family reunion. Her work was going to be even more challenging than she had anticipated.

But when the day of the reunion came, all of her relatives had worked so hard in preparing themselves that the critical woman could not find one thing about them, their clothes, the food, their children's behavior, or anything else, to criticize. She did take one minute before dinner to show her corrections on the note of response to her list, and everyone did listen and watch very closely. But after that it was a pure and happy celebration. And how could it have been otherwise, everyone realized, now that they had corrected everything that might stand in the way of their having fun!

The
Low Bridge

The county road supervisor was a pretty stupid fellow, elected by softhearted people who thought they were voting him into a harmless job.

But the first thing that man did on his new job was order construction of a road bridge that was so low it was sure to cause trouble. The problem was not so much that water flooded over it in spring thaws, but that huge pieces of ice caught on it and made terrible ice jams.

The softhearted voters saw their mistake and four years later elected a new road supervisor with more sense, but they could not elect a new bridge.

So they had to live with spring ice jams. And what happened was that every spring men in the neighborhood near the low bridge started getting this feeling when the river ice would break up and cause an ice jam. The right time to go down to the bridge just came on them like hunger, and they would go down there with picks and poles and keep the ice moving.

Hey, Jack. Hey, Bill, Arnold, you too? They surprised themselves in this way as they came together onto the bridge at the same time to free the ice.

But after a few years the ice fighters did not surprise each other or anyone else. Everyone out there had come to depend on them. Don't worry, people would remind each other. The ice men aren't out yet. We have plenty of time to plant our potatoes. And when the ice men did appear on the bridge, people got out their garden tools and spring cleaning supplies.

In one way or another the low bridge changed things for everyone out there. People were more relaxed and comfortable with life now that they had one thing they could always depend on like that. Some people felt that they slept better now and everyone was friendlier to each other. After several years a new wing was put on the old senior citizens' home because people were living longer. Young people in that community also tended to take up their family business now instead of going off to California or Boston. Nobody said out loud that they thought the low bridge had done all of these things, but everyone could remember the year that things started to get better. It was even rumored among a few of the old-timers that ducks in those parts had started counting on the ice men too and would not fly north until they saw the ice men on the low bridge. And it was perhaps no coincidence that groundhogs had gone out of style in that part of the country as predictors of spring.

Of course, what happened out there did not make that stupid road supervisor smart. Once, someone asked him, If you had to do it over again, would you?

I'd have to cross that bridge when I came to it, said the stupid man, smiling the rather predictable smile that now was so common in that community.

The
New Minister

The new minister had just arrived from the old country. He spoke with an accent but knew English well and was a wonderful preacher. The congregation liked the way he rolled his r's and the way he could make them feel guilty and relieved in the same sermon, first by pointing out how great their sins and miseries were and then by pointing the way for deliverance from those sins and miseries. He was a big hit, but sometimes his words did not come out right during congregational prayer.

One Sunday he was praying for the church's missionaries in Nigeria. What he said in his loud, deep voice, was, Lord, may it be Thy will to protect our missionaries in Nigger-ia.

There was an unwritten rule in that church that nobody would ever laugh in the sanctuary. And nobody did laugh at that. But then there was the time that he was praying and meant to say, Lord, deliver us poor sinners from the fiery darts of the Evil One. But this time, what he said was, Lord, deliver us poor sinners from the direy farts of the Evil One.

Some people coughed in their handkerchiefs. Others made sounds that could have passed for penitent sobbing. Mothers pinched their children so hard that they felt more like crying than snickering.

The minister paused only a second, and then went on, But, O Lord, not our will but Thine be done—which, people figured, was his way of apologizing for the slip of his tongue.

After church, people agreed that the Evil One had indeed made His way into the very sanctuary of the Lord. But in spite of His trickery played on the minister's tongue, everyone in the congregation had managed to bite theirs and not one real chuckle had been heard by anyone. And over that fact, everyone had a good laugh.

❀

The One
with Smelly
Armpits

His closets were filled with different kinds of deodorant sprays and roll-ons and soaps—many of them sent to him by anonymous donors but most of them bought with his own money. No one joked about the smell any more. They were calling it a disease.

Why does he wear such loud colorful clothes? everyone asked. Doesn't he know he calls enough attention to himself already? And it seems as if he wears new clothes every day!

But the one with smelly armpits was just doing everything he could to deal with his problem. The smell in the clothes he had worn more than once was too much even for him. Wearing new shirts was the least he could do—for himself, and for everyone else! And as for the bright colors, well, the one with smelly armpits had this superstition that if he wore clothing the color of bright flowers he would start smelling like bright flowers.

But the smell of his armpits followed him through the years. He was ridiculed, ostracized, spit at. And women complain of having "the curse" once a month, he mumbled despairingly to a skin graft specialist who confessed that he thought he could not help him. Have you considered solitude?

It was solitude that he finally settled on. No more bright shirts. No more special diets. No more high-powered deodorants. This is terminal, he said to himself, and it is my problem. I am going to shut myself off from the world and live alone with my stench.

But oddly enough, soon after he began his self-imposed quarantine, the world would not let him alone. Dermatologists and psychiatrists and dietitians and cosmetics representatives were calling him almost every day. They all had their reasons, most of them proclaiming humanitarian or scientific purposes. What are you going to do? he asked them sharply. Send people before and after smells of my armpits?

But one doctor was an alarmist. If this disease should spread, he cautioned, it could reach epidemic proportions and affect the psychological and physical well-being of the whole nation. It may even have defense implications, he warned.

So here I am, stinking up the space I inhabit and threatening to contaminate the whole world. I am the armpit of the universe!

It should be no surprise that it was this statement which saved him. It became a slogan. And like so many slogans forgave the very ill it celebrated. Does he meet his claim? people challenged. They came for miles to find out, and for the first time that he could remember, the one with smelly armpits disappointed no one.

Pink Curlers

The woman was so beautiful that when she went downtown she put large pink curlers in her hair to keep men from staring at her.

When men saw her like this they looked right past her slim body with its many curves and angles and right past her soft oval face. All they saw were the large pink curlers peering over her skull like so many blank faces.

Did you see that? a man would ask.

But already the other men would be walking in the opposite direction, so repelled were they by the sight of the pink curlers.

And so the woman moved safely about her errands as the men were distracted from her beauty by her large pink curlers. When she returned home, she let her hair down and brushed it out into its full and lustrous auburn waves. Her

husband would come home from his work to find her looking her best. What have I done, he often asked, to deserve
this beauty? The woman enjoyed her husband's attention,
but as the years passed and he became increasingly more
adoring of her, she realized she would have to protect herself from him too. So she started wearing pink curlers
around the house and soon his eyes too were drawn from her
beauty to the stack of curlers on her head. There came the
day when looking at her reminded him of a Gatling gun.
After that, every day when he came home from work all he
could see when he looked at her was the Gatling gun aimed
right at him.

Soon the husband left her. At last! she thought. I can let
my hair down again! But when she did, she found her
beauty was so great that she could do nothing but stare at
herself in the mirror. This frightened her so much that she
quickly put her curlers back in. And so the woman lived
happily, though alone, with her hair full of pink curlers for
the rest of her life.

Who
Always Came
Early

People started to give him the wrong time when they invited him to dinner or to a party. They would say, Be here at nine o'clock sharp, please, when they were telling everyone else eight o'clock. This way they could be sure he would arrive with the others instead of an hour early. But soon the man who always came early noticed that some people were getting there at the same time he was—or even earlier. This worried him so much that he started to come an hour and a half early.

Finally a kind but blunt woman asked him, Why do you always come early? Don't you know that people are starting to give you the wrong time just to make sure that you don't arrive while they are doing dishes or vacuuming the living room?

I knew it! shouted the man who always came early. If I had been prompt people would not have had time to sit around scheming ways to fool me!

Who
Flossed Her
Teeth in Public

It was like forgetting to put the lid on the blender.

Nothing can get in those little cracks like dental floss, she would say. As if anything else would want to.

Then she would wipe the floss clean with a napkin and roll it into a little doughnut shape on her index finger. She would put the used dental floss in a metal pillbox and tuck it back in her purse. I don't like to reuse the floss, she would say, but I like to have some extra in an emergency.

One evening as she was flossing her teeth at a large dinner party, a little girl pointed and said, Look! That lady is snowing from her mouth!

Looks more like sparks from a grindstone, said a blacksmith.

I'd say it's the beginning stages of a volcano, said a geologist.

It's fireworks! shouted the city official in charge of holiday entertainment.

Is it perhaps a new musical instrument? inquired a futurist as he stepped closer to watch the lady moving the floss between her teeth at a furious rhythmic pace.

It's clean teeth! shouted the flosser with a wet strand of floss dangling down her chin. Doesn't anyone understand? It's clean teeth! Clean teeth! Clean teeth!

Who Chewed
with His Mouth
Open

Apples were the worst. But at least they were seasonal. Peanuts were next, and they were on the grocery shelves all year.

His wife put up with the sounds of his chewing, even though those meals which most needed silence were the loudest. Like dinner the day after a funeral or right after a big fight. But she was a patient one. She was a good listener.

And for years she smiled at the sounds of his open-mouthed chewing. But in time it was no smiling matter. His manners began to turn her stomach. Even as she was preparing meals, she started to imagine the sounds of his eating. The pasty sounds of his chewing bananas. The wet crackling of his chewing carrots. And the obscene slushing sounds from the way he ate yogurt. Where were my ears when he was courting me? she asked herself many years too late. I would rather he went to the toilet with the bathroom door open. But to the wife love meant silent acceptance of a partner's habits, so she did not speak to him about his chewing.

Years passed like so many masticated meals, and in time his habit started to eat at her health. Her lips grew tight and wrinkled like dried peach halves. Her skin took on the texture of decaying pumpkin shells. She knew she could not continue her vow of loving silence.

Please, she said one sultry evening as he was squeaking his way through ripe olives—his favorites—would you please close your mouth when you are eating? The sounds are killing me.

I thought you would never ask, he said. I have been waiting for years for the chance to prove to you how much I love you.

The Flaw

Like most parents, they tried not to notice. Or they noticed it but pretended that it would go away. These sorts of problems straighten themselves out with time, they said.

The boy was not so sure about this. When other boys pointed and laughed, he figured it was forever. Every morning he would look down, and it had not changed. It hung there like a blunt fishhook, the point pointed up at his face as if accusing him of their shared predicament. Going to the bathroom, to avoid arching into the air, he sat down on the toilet and turned the end down.

But this was not the worst of his problems. When, like other boys, he reached the age of discovering pleasure with himself, the flaw grew in his hand. Now it was more like a boomerang than a blunt hook. Combined with his stomach, it was an isosceles triangle. With time, like the sharp peak of a mountain growing smooth from the caressing of wind and rain, the sharp angle grew smooth from his touch. By the time the boy was sixteen, his flaw was like a horseshoe when he was aroused, the free end clamped tightly to his belly.

The boy did not tell his parents that the flaw was still with him. And, indeed, during the normal times of work and play, there is no way that they could have known. They believed their son must have outgrown his flaw long ago. Nor did they worry when their son started to get fat. This, too, they thought, was one of his passing flaws. And when he showed no interest in girls, they assumed that one problem had led to another and that he would find an interest in girls as soon as he lost some weight. Everything in due time, they said.

What the parents did not know is that the boy figured he would only have himself to turn to in what could be a long life. The fat of his stomach provided him with his greatest pleasure. When he had reached grand proportions of obesity, he would often go off by himself and his complementary flaws. When he was fully aroused, his huge stomach seemed to part for him like the walls of water in the Red Sea, giving him a deep and tempting opening, which he entered with great though silent rejoicing.

The
New Family

One day a new family moved into the neighborhood. They did not go to church and no one knew their nationality.

The neighbor ladies first figured there was going to be a problem with this family when on Monday mornings there was hardly any wash on their clothesline. Just a few towels. Something is missing here, they said and started asking around if anyone knew anything about this unusual new family.

But it was the boys who first discovered what was really different about the new family. They walked over and looked through the windows. The new family did not wear any clothing. Not the father, mother, sister, or brother.

After the boys told their story many grown-ups found ways of getting a look at the new family too. Maybe they have some kind of skin disease, suggested one woman who liked to believe the best about people.

But the naked family looked pretty healthy to everyone who got a look at them, and soon teenage boys were driving their cars by at night and honking or whistling when they saw the naked wife.

Some women got together and decided something should be done before the whole community was in a turmoil. So they appointed a committee of women who were good talkers to go and see the new family and let them know about the problems they were causing. It never occurred to them that the naked husband would answer the door.

The women were so embarrassed to see a naked man standing there that they either stared at the ground or tried to look only at his face. They all blushed brightly.

Seeing the women's shame, the man reached behind the door and handed them some black scarves which he had hanging there. Here, he said. Put these over your faces. It will make you feel more comfortable.

The women did not dare to refuse the naked man. They put the black scarves over their faces so that they could not see him.

There is a problem in the neighborhood, said one of the women from beneath her black scarf.

Really, said the naked man. Where is it?

We can't see it right now, said the woman.

Very well then, said the naked man. I am happy I could help you. You may keep those scarves for as long as you need them.

Three Women
Were in
the Café

Three women were in the café talking about what they were eating.

Mmm, this sandwich is delicious, said one woman. She opened it to show the other women the vegetables that were inside. Would you like a taste? she asked.

The second woman reached toward the sprouts and avocado with her fork.

Oh, use your fingers, said the woman with the sandwich.

Would you like to taste my oyster stew? said the third woman. It is very buttery. And you must try my salad, said the second woman. The house dressing is wonderful!

To make the sharing easier, the women passed their trays around the table.

When they finished eating all the food, the women argued over the check. They all wanted to pay for all three because each of them felt she had eaten the most. My stomach is so full, I should pay, said one. Oh, no, said the second. I eat so fast I know I had the most. My mouth is twice as big as both of yours put together, said the third. Let me take the check.

They all laid money on the table and it was far too much. But as the first woman was emptying her pockets, the second said, What a lovely coat. Oh, yes, said the first. This cotton lining is so soft on the skin. Here, do try it on. What about that velour sweater? she asked the third. Mauve is my favorite color. Oh, try it on, said the third woman. Are those boots new?

And so the women started exchanging clothes, helping each other with the buttons and snaps. Some of the articles did not fit the other women very well, but by this time the women had become expert at working out the minor details.

Three Doctors

Three doctors were sailing in the bay. The winds were strong, but no match for their skill as sailors.

The surgeon was tending the sheets. Let me take that, said the general practitioner. If you get a finger caught in the winch, you're out of business.

All right, said the surgeon, taking the tiller.

Keep an eye on the jib, said the GP. If it jibes, the main's next.

No sweat, said the surgeon.

Everything seems to be under control, said the psychiatrist and went below for the bourbon.

They sat back to relax. They sipped their bourbon. They started to chat.

How have things been at the office? the surgeon asked the GP.

Oh, all right, but we are having a harder time collecting than ever before.

Same problem, said the surgeon.

Same here, said the psychiatrist. I wonder how people imagine the world can continue to function when they can't take care of the simple matter of paying their bills.

I don't know. I don't know either, said the other two.

I had one woman said that having therapy taught her not to worry about money, said the psychiatrist. She said the money was my worry and maybe I should see a psychiatrist.

My god, said the general practitioner. Though I had a case that was just as bad. This woman called me on the phone so she wouldn't have the expense of an office call. She said she was into preventative medicine. Wanted me to recommend ways to care for her children so they wouldn't get sick. I suggested a balanced diet, lots of sleep, and instilling a positive outlook on life. I figured this is what she wanted to hear. Next week all three of her kids had the flu. She came in with them and not only expected a free office call but free drugs. She said that was the least I could do for the bad advice.

My god, said the psychiatrist.

Listen to this one, said the surgeon. I had one welfare mother wanted to barter me some painted gourds for her back surgery. She said she spent twelve hours painting them—that she wouldn't charge me for the seeds and the planting and the rest of the gardening. She figured we were even. She said, I put in four hours for you for every one you put in for me, and that should be fair!

Something is going to have to change, that's for sure, said the psychiatrist.

You can say that again, said the GP.

Sooner or later, said the psychiatrist. The world can't go on like this forever, that's for sure.

The blocks creaked as the doctors brought the stern into the eye of the wind and hauled in the mainsheet.

Ready? said the surgeon.

Ready, said the GP.

Jibe-o, said the surgeon.

The mainsail snapped over and the boat shivered slightly as it crossed the wind.

Okay. Main out, said the GP.

Piece of cake, said the surgeon.

Piece of cake, said the psychiatrist, setting up another round.

The Ones
You Don't See

One night a tornado was spotted and everyone went out on the schoolground where they would have a good view.

It's the ones you don't see that get you, said one old man who had lived around there for sixty-five years.

The tornado waved in the sky like a torn hem on a black skirt, still several miles west of where the people were watching. It grew thinner as they watched and then touched down and looked as if it exploded where it met the earth. As it came closer everyone heard it—like a big broom sweeping across gravel.

It's the ones you don't hear that get you, said the old man, still showing no fear of the tornado. But he was the only one on the schoolground who was not scared. Take cover! a young father yelled. We'll all be killed!

His voice cut through the sound of the approaching tornado and everyone ran to their cars, or to their homes if they lived close by.

The old man waited until the tornado was almost close enough to take off his shirt before he lifted the cover of the abandoned schoolhouse cistern. He slid down and pulled the lid over himself as he had done during the last three tornadoes which had struck in that same area.

The story only a few people know is of the old woman who was out there on the schoolground too. When the tornado got close, she said in a loud whisper, My diamonds! My diamonds! Then she waddled home in her own shaggy way. And while her bachelor son who lived with her was coaxing their dogs into the root cellar near their house, she gathered her six tiny diamonds from their hiding place in the kitchen cupboard, just as she had done many times before when she thought they were in danger—like the time young boys were threatening to break into her house on Halloween night; or the time she woke from a nightmare in which atomic bombs were falling—she took her six diamonds and, one at a time, swallowed them.

As she then hurried from the kitchen toward the basement door, she glanced out a window to see her son close the root cellar door safely behind him and the dogs. And above him, in midair, like so many wingless pigeons, flew a small herd of young pigs in the midst of churning straw and splintered lumber, spinning crazily upward. She moved safely into the basement as the roof of her house opened like a mouth. She stumbled across the basement floor and rolled under a butcher block which remained standing while the tornado inhaled the surroundings.

The next day neighbors came out through the wreckage as proud of their stories of survival as they were humbled by what the tornado had taken.

While the old man still chattered on in his senile way about the ways of tornadoes in those parts, the grateful and quiet old woman picked her diamonds from her excrement with a tweezers which had remained safe in her loose apron pocket.

Weekends

When Mulligan the town midget was a boy, he wanted to join the circus. His ordinary-sized parents would hear nothing of it. They did not want people saying their son was a freak who had to join the circus. So Mulligan learned to repair shoes instead. He worked hard at it and made a decent living, but by the time Mulligan was only twenty-three it was no secret that he drank too much beer.

The biggest problem for Mulligan was that he loved people. So on weekends, instead of drinking at home, he liked to go to the crowded poolroom and join the rowdy men in the fun. He was too short to play pool, but the men gave him beers for racking the balls. He stood on a stool and did the job nicely, but he did not hold his beer well. After only three glasses he was so drunk that he would drop pool balls and slur his words.

That is when the men knew it was time to help Mulligan outside because another beer or two would make him vomit and ruin the game for everyone. One of the men would carry him out to a bench in front of the hardware store. It was called Mulligan's Bench.

Once Mulligan was on his bench, his troubles were not over, because on weekend nights teenage boys prowled the streets. The same boys whose shoes he had repaired would find him on his bench nearly passed out. They would make a half-circle around him so that people driving by could not see what was happening. Then they would unbutton Mulligan's fly and masturbate him. This brought him back to his senses, but seeing the size and number of teenage boys made Mulligan pretend not to notice.

When the boys finished, they would leave laughing and Mulligan would fall asleep.

Weekend nights were also a bad time for the town night watchman, a crippled man who was no match for the rowdy boys. But he did his job, and with the same dedication that he checked the store doors he also checked Mulligan's fly.

The same God who made midgets made weekends, he would say to himself as he tucked Mulligan in and buttoned him up before continuing on his monotonous rounds.

The Graveyard
Story

There was a fight over whether to make the graveyard larger. The fight started between the mayor and the farmer who owned the land around the graveyard and would not sell. The farmer came to town council meetings, and he and the mayor argued in front of everyone.

Keep your creeping graveyard to yourselves, the farmer said. You city people have already taken enough land with houses and roads.

There are only ten slots left, explained the mayor. What kind of person is it who would punish the dead?

The farmer was a bit more clever than the mayor and made jokes about beating dead horses and letting the dead bury their dead, but within a week there were only six slots left. When this news made the headlines, no one died for six weeks. The old people seemed to be holding their breath for fear that they might have to be cremated or shipped out of town to be buried.

The farmer's land was zoned agricultural. Before it could be used for a graveyard, it would have to be rezoned as Residential II, and the mayor was working on that. He figured he could force the farmer to sell if the taxes were high enough.

It was an election year, and the mayor was afraid he would lose if the graveyard were not expanded soon. Now the farmer accused him of running on a graveyard ticket, and there were many letters to the editor suggesting different ways the mayor could solve the graveyard problem. There were cartoons showing triple-decker burials and high-rise tombs. There was a pre-death starvation diet to make people thinner so they would take up less space.

Then the campaign got to be too much for the mayor and he had a heart attack. The farmer went one step too far when he accused the mayor of having a heart attack as a campaign gimmick to show how much more space in the graveyard was needed. People thought the farmer was being cruel and so they backed the mayor, reelected him and helped pass a new zoning ordinance which made the farmer's land Residential II. The farmer did have to sell, but at a very good price.

Everyone seemed relieved that the fight was over, and a dozen old people died within a week. Now people joked about the farmer for cashing in on what they called Death Futures. The mayor recovered, but he pointed out that the graveyard had only been expanded by ten acres. It's a stopgap measure, he said, but life is not made up of permanent solutions.

Design by David Bullen
Typeset in Mergenthaler Imprint
and Cochin display
by Wilsted & Taylor
Printed by Maple-Vail
on acid-free paper